THINKS

Keith Waterhouse

THINKS

MICHAEL JOSEPH
LONDON

First published in Great Britain by Michael Joseph Ltd
44 Bedford Square, London WC1
1984

British Library Cataloguing in Publication Data
Waterhouse, Keith
    Thinks.
    I. Title
    823'.914[F]   PR6073.A82

ISBN 0 7181 2329 8

Typeset by Rowland Phototypesetting Ltd,
Bury St Edmunds, Suffolk

Printed and bound in Great Britain by
Billing and Sons Ltd, Worcester

I

There's your man – the one with his lips moving.

That one across from the two yobs sprawled over four seats, yobbishly swigging cans of lime 'n' lemon while they plot how to screw another year out of the education-grant cornucopia by applying for some useless time-wasting yob course he can't quite gather what.

He has a plan to saw their legs off. An anaesthetic dart job it would have to be – obviously he'd have accomplices, they'd be a gang: the League of Justice, something of the sort. One, masked by his *Financial Times*, would blow the dart. Phut, phut, twice. Another, a surgeon, would perform the operation there and then with a laser apparatus. The carriage would have to be otherwise empty, that goes without saying. His own role would be to pin a tastefully-printed card, SEATS ARE FOR SITTING ON, to their yobbish chests, and alight at East Croydon with their sawn-off legs in a plastic bin-liner. Bound to be a builder's skip handy.

He's Edgar Samuel Bapty, as sane as anyone on this 8.33 from Portsea to Victoria, except when he's overweight. That's when his blood pressure goes up and he thinks vicious thoughts. He's thinking another one now: it concerns the swining bloody-minded ticket collector on platform four who refused to let him through the unattended left-hand barrier on the grounds that it was supposed to be an exit, so forcing him to join the long queue filtering through the right-hand barrier. That wasn't today, it was about eight weeks ago. Bapty would like to get that sod's name and have it read out on the Portsea Sound breakfast programme, together with an apology from the Railways Board for their pig-faced employee's unauthorised over-zealousness.

That swining bloody-minded pig-faced snot-gobbling attendant at the Harbour Mall car park, refusing to part with change for the pay-and-display machine, they could have him on too. An interview. *So you've no specific instructions from the council to refuse to give change, it's just part of your own general policy of getting up the ratepayers' noses?* Awkward Squad, the spot could be called.

Do the workings of Bapty's mind interest you at all? There is nothing spectacularly untoward about it – no big brain functioning there, nor malfunctioning either, come to that: no particular behavioural quirks, no Jekyll and Hyde fighting it out. Bapty is no more a cerebral freak than that woman in front or the couple behind or the two yobs across the aisle or any of those clerks and secretaries behind their crosswords and horoscopes and thick paperbacks: their thoughts, were you privy to them, would very likely, given the special circumstances of Bapty's day (and of Bapty's blood pressure) prove as ordinarily unusual or as extraordinarily commonplace as his.

What does set Bapty's mind off from all others, so far as you are concerned, is that you are able to look into it, as through a window. Even that is not unique – if you are a reader of novels to any extent, like all these commuting typists, you must have seen into other people's minds often enough. But Bapty exists in the flesh, and he does not know that you are doing as you would do if he existed only on paper. It is a game you are playing on him. There are rules to this game, which you must follow closely. Break them, and it could be dangerous. But so long as you adhere to them, you may eavesdrop on all Bapty's thoughts today.

See his lips moving again.

– Madam (he is thinking), could you kindly control that child?

There is no child in this carriage. Bapty is rehearsing what he would have himself say were one fidgeting opposite, kicking his knees.

Watch him now as he rises and makes for the buffet car, already, in his head, tapping coins on laminate as he addresses the swining bone-idle bastardising steward skulking in his pantry:

— Could we have some service here, my friend, or are you at your devotions?

You may follow Edgar Bapty if you wish, but not too closely.

See how he postures in the dark blue velvet suit too tight for his build, too datedly stylish for his age, which is fifty. *Gear*, he still calls it, to himself though not to others, much of his mental vocabulary being stuck in the sixties. He imagines that the glance that office girl gives him, as he passes down the carriage with a swagger that is almost a waddle, is one of admiration. You, who saw her mouth twitching, know otherwise. He must not become aware of your awareness.

These are the rules. You must never get near enough to overhear what he is saying aloud or what is being said to him, though all other things being equal you should usually be near enough to lip-read his thoughts. You may keep him under observation, however, only in public or semi-public places: a restaurant (provided you are at separate tables) but not a private banqueting suite, a general office (but stay out of earshot) though not a private office, Dr Windows' waiting room, not Dr Windows' surgery — while Bapty is undergoing his check-up this morning, you will just have to be patient and read a magazine. Better, even, if he gives you time, pick up a paperback at Victoria: considering all he has programmed for himself today, there may be one or two long waits.

No listening at doors: and anyway Bapty's thoughts cannot transmit through wood, glass or walls.

— Oh, there you are, steward! I was beginning to think this was British Rail's answer to the *Marie Celeste*.

Now this may take a little getting used to. Notice how his lips moving don't synchronise with what you're hearing. Nor does his demeanour to the steward — affability bordering upon the grovelling — square with the seething hatred he feels for the swining bone-idle bastardising pig-faced snot-gobbler for having kept him waiting eleven seconds. There will be a lot of this. You will hear not what he actually says, which as often as not is of little interest, but what he would like to say. It should give you a more accurate perception of Edgar Samuel Bapty than the spoken platitudes and pleasantries that ease him through the day.

Cowbag. The epithet drops seemingly unbidden into his head as he turns away from the serving hatch and a signal from his searing fingers instructs him to locate a resting-place for his slopping coffee carton. Evidently it has been triggered off by that disorganised-looking woman there who looks to have taken over the buffet car like a bag-lady while she messily consumes her slab cake and tea. But it is not her selfishly hogging the whole of the one available narrow ledge with her sprawled belongings that evokes this vicious response from Bapty, although he has certainly registered both her thoughtlessness and the space deficiency that compounds it, and indeed in a sub-stratum of his brain has called up on his mental word-processor his sarcastic standing letter to the Travellers Fare wing of British Rail or possibly *The Times* – it is in a perpetual state of revision – on the subject of buffet car design.

No: while few and far between are those to whom he would not apply some barnyard classification or another at some time or another, it is not everyone who gets to be called a cowbag by Bapty.

There must be something about her that reminds him of Margot. There can be no physical resemblance – the woman's face remains no more than a blur in his mind's eye, saving only the bright slash of lipstick. It must be her generally sluttish aura. Bapty sees with hard clarity her handbag gaping open to reveal a hoard of makeup-soiled Kleenex that could just as well have been thrown away, notes how tackily she crumbles up her fruit slice and fouls the plastic ledge with its gungy cellophane wrapper, takes in the sloppily-folded newspaper and jumble of knitting, clothing accessories and magazines in the scuffed canvas tote bag at her feet, but fails, to his annoyance, to track

8

down the cigarette packet that would condemn her of being about to use her paper plate as an ashtray. *Cowbag*. Unknown to its surrogate victim, the taunt flicks and sears like a gob of acid spittle. *Cowbag*. Even though it's been a good two years now. Never let it be said of Bapty that he is a man to forgive and forget. Far from it: incubating all his grudges from the first pre-foetal murmur, real or imagined, he has a phenomenal memory both for slights yet to be perpetrated and revenge still to be exacted.

– Do you know what you are, Margot? I've been wanting to tell you this for a very long time . . .

But he never has done. That passing fragment is from the twelve-minute epitaph he composed following her departure. Barely two minutes in its first draft, it became longer and longer as he honed and polished it on furious back-and-forth walks along the harbour wall, arms flailing, lips moving. How Bapty wishes he could apothecarise a concentrate of all that venom into a pellet and insert it into her brain, like a bee-sting; that she could read his mind as you reading it now.

– Though I'm keenly aware, Margot, that to compare you with to compare you to a cow's udder the udder of a cow—

(These running corrections and improvements are usual with Bapty.)

– is to disparage a useful organ the most useful organ of a noble creature. Perhaps shitbag would be nearer the mark.

He must never know that you know. He must not even suspect your presence. Therefore, even should you become temporarily confused by what is going on in Bapty's head, you must not be tempted to clarify the situation by raising questions, for all that it would probably be easy enough to infiltrate them into his consciousness in your privileged position.

Patience is called for. From time to time you may have trouble slotting what his mind is saying into its proper category – whether it is a hasty rehearsal of the speech to which he is about to give voice, or a retrospective revision of what he has just said but wishes he had put better, or a touched-up version of words once spoken either by himself or others which are unacceptable to his memory bank in their original form and so must be re-edited, or a note towards some anticipated conversation, or a contribution to a long-running, wholly imaginary dialogue or monologue, or a riposte – as to the buffet-car steward just now – that he would dearly love to deliver were he outwardly the same man as he is inwardly; or any one of a hundred other possibilities; or any permutation thereof. Nor, time not being of the essence in the world of Bapty's head, will you necessarily be certain whether what you come across in there is in the real or imagined or doctored past, the existing although possibly anaesthetised present, the anticipated or utopian future, or the timeless zone of pipe-dreams, neuroses and euphoria. There will be clues in plenty, but you cannot always rely on them – where Bapty is hellbent on pulling the wool over his own eyes for whatever reason, he may well succeed in pulling it over yours. You will have to judge as best you are able what is real and what is not, while at the same time weighing up, as the assayer of Bapty's mind, whether the real is any more real than the unreal or the half-real, or indeed, on occasion, even less real.

Do you wonder why you are playing this game? Why not? Is there some other game you would sooner be playing? It can do no harm – provided you do not forget the rules – and the exercise may even do you good.

– Buggerisation British Telecom.

Now here is a case in point. Is Bapty – prompted, perhaps, by the telegraph poles flashing by – making a general case against the telephone service, or a particular one? Is his point of reference some actual past incident or mish-mash of several past incidents, or an expected future experience based on past experience or the exaggeration of past experience, either accumulative or isolated, or an invented or partly-invented or at least hand-tinted past experience, governing present expectations, should he have such a thing as a phone call in mind? Or what?

Take the likeliest bet. Did this *Buggerisation British Telecom* thought-flash start out as a routine reminder to himself that there is someone he has to ring when he reaches Victoria, then become distorted, corrupted, by a fear that he will find the pay-phone out of order? Listen:

– Sir: Bearing in mind the immense strides made in the field of telecommunications in recent years, it seems unlikely that an unbreakable telephone remains beyond our technological capabilities. One can only assume that British Telecom pursues a policy of built-in obsolescence in order to provide employment for—

One of his stock letters to *The Times*. He won't send it – he won't even write it. That phone call hunch was right, though. The name *Ruth, Ruth* now washing up like driftwood on the beach of his conscious mind indicates to whom the call has to be made – though not its purpose, nor who this Ruth might be. You will have to wait for that. Her name bobs away on the ebb-tide, to be at once submerged as the next crashing wave pounds into Bapty's skull the wish that he could catch a phone vandal red-handed. The yob's dead eyes are reincarnated by terror as looming shadows and the reflection of glinting scalpels prompt him to look up from his yobbish handiwork, and find himself in the hands of The League of Justice.

A service message next, as the train stops on a signal. Bapty routinely sweats: going to be late. *British Piss-piddling Rail regret any inconvenience to passengers due to delay caused by signal failure at*— It's all right: moving again. He consults his watch. On time, should be.

The next matter on Bapty's agenda is whether he should pee now, directly he's finished his coffee, or hold out until Victoria. The voice of Dr Windows, as he scribbles a prescription, is summoned into being:

– Now if you take these as often as you should, Mr Bapty, there'll probably be an effect on your waterworks, so try not to take so many fluids on board, eh? Especially of the alcoholic variety.

To which Bapty replies, or claims to reply:

– Hairy spherical objects.

If he pees now he could comfortably fit in one more pee in a pub before his interview with Metropolitan Cable, whereas if he saves it up for Victoria he might not want to go in the pub and so would be running the risk of the need coming on again during the interview itself. Perhaps he should compromise and wait until the train is pulling out of East Croydon. The pros and cons occupy him pretty well exclusively for nigh on twenty seconds – a light-year in the galaxy of Bapty's mind.

Curious that the interview has only just now resurfaced, and only so peripherally, considering that it was in trepidation of it that he awoke clammily at dawn, when he began to marshal his anticipated responses only to drift off at once into day-dreams of sex across his desk with the lustful young divorcee he wouldn't mind having as his secretary in the remote event of young Jepcott regarding him as anything other than a clapped-out old fart who ought to be applying for early retirement, never mind a new job. It's all in there somewhere, of course – not only his heavily-edited curriculum vitae but also a comprehensive career portfolio including his letter of appointment to MetCable TV, his letter of resignation from Portsea Sound, the trade press release, the interview in the *Portsea Chronicle*, and much of the text of young Jepcott's speech at the staff Christmas dinner, wherein he joshingly recalls his doubts in respect of Bapty's age, experience and capabilities. In the same file – Exhibit B, if you like – is a crisp note signed Ralph Jepcott Chief Executive, thanking Bapty for coming up to London and giving of his time but regretting that the post has been filled elsewhere. Another, softer version regrets that because of economies the post has had to be filled in-house. There is also the rough transcript of such scrappy pre-recollections of the interview as Bapty permits to survive.

For the present, though, the whole dossier is suppressed, and he would prefer to keep it that way until it is all over. *Screwed that one, Bapty, didn't you, old son?* he can then tell himself. His rueful self-reproaches are on file too, ready for immediate release once the embargo has been lifted. He really ought to be thinking seriously about that interview, though. It'll surface soon enough now, you'll see.

He finishes his coffee, looks for a bin or basket in which to dispose of his disposable beaker and being disappointed to find one, transfers his grudge back to the swining bone-idle pox-bollocking steward for failing to pick up a used plastic spoon where it lies in a pool of tea on the unwiped counter. Moving on out of the buffet car, Bapty wishes in passing that the Chairman of British Rail were a fellow member of Portsea Golf Club – though whether he is himself a member, his mind does not make clear. Possibly not, for he drops the theme at once.

Cross your fingers and hope he isn't about to have been at school with the General Manager, Southern Region. Those conversations can get rather tedious. You can, however, always switch off for a period, as you would a radio, just so long as Bapty does not, so to speak, hear the click, and by realising that there is no-one any longer listening, perceive that someone has been.

There is one more rule, or rather a condition, on this voyage. Bapty's mental bilges, while they may momentarily slop up through the deep hold of his unconsciousness on occasion, are to be regarded as out of bounds. Monitoring the aborted, unformed images and swirling Joycean word-associations that are discharged like gas with every breath and heartbeat, the slipstream effluent of bowel movements, blood and maggots and dark secrets, would be as exhausting as trying to log the millionth-of-a-second by millionth-of-a-second progress of an atomic clock, as well as being mightily unpleasant. Besides, that is not the game.

What is the game, then?

Consider how you would explain it to Edgar Samuel Bapty were he to rumble what you were up to. He mustn't – but if he did?

You could only take the bull by the horns, explaining boldly that you are entitled to tap his mind because in that dimension he is no more than fiction – so unrecognisably different from flesh-and-blood Bapty, so much not what Bapty would admit to being, and so lacking in substance or status, that unless this mind-Bapty is Bapty's soul (and God help Bapty if he is) then

13

never mind that the fiction gives you a greater insight than the facts ever could – he is as corporeally and spiritually non-existent as a character in a book.

You could go on to plead that you have meticulously respected the physical Bapty's right to his own private conversations because they expose facets of his material life, which is none of your business. You could mention your resolve to keep just as scrupulously out of the wastes of his unconsciousness, knowing that to have intruded there would have been to reveal things he dare not even face himself, let alone parade in public. You have trespassed only in his invented mind. Unless Bapty wished to invoke the copyright laws to protect his each and every thought as he thinks it (and there is no legal precedent) he would be left without a case. He is, like everyone, living a novel, and you are doing no more than read it over his shoulder.

2

That slick of blackish-red splashing across the printout of his mind like spilled ink on a page is boiling rage, generated by the young man in the blue velvet suit perilously identical to his own, who about to enter the buffet car just as he is about to leave it, stands aside with what Bapty regards as condescending courtesy to let him through.

You will remember that office girl along the train smirking at Bapty's 'gear.' You saw it, he didn't. This time he sees a smirk where you don't. More than likely he sees what is not there: the young man, carrying a universe of his own on those slim shoulders, has his own thoughts to think. But if he does register Bapty by virtue of coincidentally wearing the same kind of suit, he could conceivably be noting – smirkingly – how incongruously flashy it looks on an older man, not realising that Bapty is in a branch of show business and therefore simply wearing the uniform of his trade. Bapty, as he brushes past with a pleasant nod, tries to brand the information with hot irons into the young man's brain. Recognising that the message has not got through, he seizes his tormentor by his velvet lapels and, addressing him as Sunny Jim, enquires what it feels like to be nothing but a tinpot little, piss-piddling little, rectum-crawling wages clerk.

The young man briefly smiles, acknowledging Bapty's nod. To Bapty, it was a sneer.

To reassure himself, he mentally looks in a mirror, which being a version of Snow White's produces a reflection of himself as he was on the other side of forty, slimmer then where he might admit to a certain stockiness now, the wide-striped shirt more at the height of fashion – *with it* as they used to say and as Bapty still does, though not aloud – the suede shoes unscuffed and unstained in those days when he could hold a glass steadier, the dandruff less of a problem. Perhaps dark blue velvet was a mistake after all. Swatting a speckled shoulder he unexpectedly, self-pityingly, glimpses himself in a different, non-magic glass – a smoke-clouded pub mirror – and observing a resemblance to a second-hand car salesman specialising in used Cortinas, hates the young man for probably mistaking him for one, and smirking.

Bapty blunders on through the train, smirking himself now at a cruel fancy. Already contracts manager of Metropolitan Cable, he is considering applications for the post of his assistant. The young man in the duplicate of Bapty's velvet suit is on his way up to Town to be interviewed as Bapty's prospective junior, even as Bapty himself, on the ephemeral plane of his true existence, is on his way up to Town to be interviewed as his prospective junior's prospective senior.

– Come in, son, sit yourself down. Good of you to come. We've met somewhere, haven't we? Trade fair reception, was it?

– I don't think so, sir.

– You mean you don't think we've met, or you don't think it was at the trade fair, which?

– I don't think we've met.

– But you're not sure. That's a bloody good start, I must say. I seem to have made about as much impression as the Invisible Man.

There's a lot more of this cat-and-mouse dialogue already structured – it must be an adaptation of one of his old scripts – but Bapty, impatient for the kill, now jumps to the punchline:

– I'll remind you, shall I? The 8.33 from Portsea this morning. To be more precise, in the doorway of the buffet car . . .

No: too bland. Revenge is savoury, not sweet, with Bapty. A mutilation tableau, one of a series he keeps in stock like prints of the Seven Stages of Cruelty, replaces the cosy little playlet, disturbing, even disgusting him, for a second or two. He shouldn't allow his head to give houseroom to that sort of thing. Bapty exorcises the scene by the device of scattering nonsense words as from a censer – *luggage bath, ample, barbecue, Preston, float-plate* – and, purged, reaches the sanctuary of his carriage just as the two yobs whose legs he would like to saw off decide to head for the buffet car.

– Oh, I should, lads, I should, before you're taken faint. It must be a good three minutes since refreshment last slid down your gullets.

He fleetingly sees blood spurting from their yobbish mouths as they yobbishly chomp potato crisps laced with broken glass. *Acorn, massive, larking, pay-bomb.* SHUT THE PIGGING DOOR! he mentally screams. They do, as a matter of fact, shut it, but Bapty believes he may be excused for assuming they wouldn't. Their discarded lime 'n' lemon cans roll towards him as he resumes his seat. They are the kind of yobs who leave empty cans spiked on railings, where he would like to spike their heads. *Scunthorpe, pepper-tone, sapling, maypole* . . . Hypnotically, the censer swings . . .

At last, after a quarter of a minute or so, a mask of tranquillity slips into place over that flayed, twitching ball of raw nerve ends that is the mind of Edgar Samuel Bapty. That old farmhouse gliding by – Jacobean, is it? He sees himself living in it: always does, every time his train passes this spot. Feeding the pigs and bringing in the eggs, then off with the wellies and into the Jag. Today there'll be Christmas turkeys for Ralph Jepcott and one or two other close colleagues.

The Christmas frost melts in the September sunlight and the farmhouse has gone now: he has mixed, like a film, to his own home in Marine Close, Portsea. Don't be taken in. Its brickwork is nowhere near as mellow as that, nor are those laburnums full-grown. Reduce its proportions by about fifty per cent, as you would through a photographic enlarger where the focus is faulty. Halve the market price you'd put on it. Edit back in the dock cranes on the horizon which he has edited out. He would make a good architect, would Bapty, the way he has drawn that street, all pleasant and leafy, with villagey-looking residents chatting by the pillar box, and just a sketched-in hint of lobster pots and yacht sails. But faintly, patchily visible through this agreeable scene, like a painted-over picture brought out by X-rays, is the reality of a cul-de-sac of newish bungalows on an estate built on reclaimed mud-flats. Legoland, he calls it, when property euphoria is not upon him.

Briefcase. Here, suddenly, it comes: the reluctant, desultory burst of thinking about that interview which he's kept putting off like the pee he's still putting off. It's sparked off by this computer-salesman type swaying through the carriage from the buffet car, scalding himself at every step with two polystyrene beakers juggled in one hand, the other being clamped to his black executive briefcase which he clutches at shoulder height for balance as if taking up the slack of some umbilical attachment.

Should Bapty have brought his briefcase, would a briefcase parked at his feet or on his lap make a favourable impression? Notwithstanding that he has left it a bit late to be asking that question, he considers it earnestly.

No, he would look as if he were selling insurance. Leave briefcase in outer office, then, and get reminded by fanciable secretary not to forget it? Give busy-busy impression of having further appointments in Town?

Further job appointments, more like. He conjures up a picture of young Jepcott – a rather one-dimensional, cardboard cut-out picture, since he knows him only by his photograph in a business magazine profile – watching sardonically from his office doorway as Bapty sweatily retrieves his quite obviously totally empty briefcase and then has to transfer it from one sweaty hand to the other before he can execute his farewell handshake.

– We'll be in touch then, Edgar. Thanks for stopping by.

Bapty has Jepcott peppering his speech with Americanisms on the authority of that magazine article, which made him sound vaguely mid-Atlantic. Probably been to New York once. Bapty can't stand him.

– My pleasure, Charles. Not Charles – Ralph.

He's going to screw this if he's not careful. Ralph. As in Richardson. Ralph Jepson. Jimsen. Jensen. Westmacott. Agatha Christie. Edgar Allan Poe. Beazley. Montgomery. Clift. Jepcott. Ralph Jepcott, Ralph Jepcott, Ralph Jepcott.

– Oh, good morning, I have an appointment with Mr James Jepmacott . . .

He has Jepcott's letter in his inside pocket. He touches it to check it's still there. He'll burn the signature into his brain immediately prior to approaching the reception desk. Jepcott. Ralph Jepcott.

– Oh, good morning, I have an appointment with Mr Ralph Jepcott. My name's Camberwell.

No, Bapty is not given to forgetting his own name. An emergency brain-swerve, that was, as a hideous, unanswerable question looms suddenly into his sights like a horn-blaring, headlight-flashing juggernaut: *Or Rafe Jepcott, does he call himself?*

In a panic, Bapty reviews the only solution available, which is not to turn up. Get off the train at East Croydon and go back to Portsea. It means skipping Dr Windows but sod that.

Why cancelling Ralph Jepcott would also involve cancelling Dr Windows, Bapty's mind is unable to tell him. It is in too much of a turmoil.

The sweat-darts pricking his forehead melt like icicles. He's calm again. Ask the MetCable receptionist, that's the answer.

He's jettisoned the briefcase dilemma by now, what with all his other anxieties connected with this interview. Here he is now sitting in Jepcott's office, arms straddling the back of a king-sized, L-shaped sofa, outwardly quite relaxed though his fingernails dig deep into the oatmeal fabric. Jepcott will be pouring coffee.

– So let me ask you this, Edgar. Any particular reason for wanting to leave Portsea Sound after what? Less than three years?

Two and three quarters. Better to ask why he took the job in the first place. Bigger fish, smaller pool. A jump up from waiting to fill a dead men's shoes at Radio Thames. And it got

Margot out of London. Got the fly out of the jampot, so he'd thought. Or hoped. The cowbag.

While musing thus, Bapty has been producing an adequate answer to Jepcott's question in some other compartment of his mind. That he does not know what he has said makes the reply no less convincing, for Jepcott seems satisfied.

– Anything else you'd like to tell us, Edgar?

– Not unless you'd like me to expand on any of my career details at all, Ralph? Rafe? I would just mention that the role of station manager in a small place like Portsea is a very different fish from what you might imagine from a big place like—

That can be improved on, surely. Bapty rewinds his celebral tape then jumps it forward to the section that needs attention:

– Mention role small place Portsea vastly different from the equivalent position at say Radio Thames, which as you may know I was next in line for, for which as you may know I was probably had a good chance of being next in line had I elected to stay there wait around long enough dead men's shoes. It's very much jack of all trades at Portsea – anything goes wrong, someone hasn't turned up let's say, you just roll up your sleeves and pitch in. Cassette library, switchboard, continuity, you name it. Great fun. I've even read the news before now.

Bapty is getting into his stride now, but he'll overdo it if he's not careful. As his small pang of embarrassment informs you (embarrassment not at telling a lie but at the prospect of it somehow leaking out that he has told it) he has never read the news in his life, though he sees himself doing it often enough. By way of going off at a pleasant tangent, he does so now. Lionel Valentine too pissed to go on, late-shift announcer nowhere to be found, Bapty steps into the breach without a tremor – *local tide times tomorrow*, he even manages to get his tongue round – then goes across to Winnie's Bar, accepts congratulatory scotch from Valentine and fires the bastard. It's one of Bapty's standbys, this sequence. He knows it so much by heart that he has got it down to a playing time of six seconds.

Here's another, with the same leading man. This one he

takes more slowly. Lionel Valentine in bed with Margot – on the bed, rather, though whose bed we are not told. Naked, not actually at it but between bouts. And both mummified with shock as Bapty throws open the door. See how incongruous they look, propped up on their elbows like fossils dug out of Pompeii. Slow fade.

Did that happen? Who is to know?

– You wouldn't find MetCable's contracts department a little on the tame side after all those excitements, Edgar?

See Bapty's lip curl. He's been waiting for this one. *Oh, no you don't, you smooth sod, Jepcott.*

– Far from it, Ralph, Rafe. It would be excitement enough getting in on the ground floor of cable TV at any level—

Ground floor at any level won't do. *In whatever role, position, department, luggage-bath,* better make that.

– Added to which I've been around contracts long enough to know the work's not as dull as it sounds. Not as routine as it sounds. Not always as routine as it sometimes sounds.

He'll play around with that later. The word *challenging* drops into the kaleidoscope of phrases he's tumbling around in his efforts to counter Jepcott's cunning insinuation that only a time-serving deadbeat would want such a boring job. *Challenging* ought to be worked in somewhere.

– And any particular reason for wanting to come to us, Edgar, or are you looking around in general?

– I've already told you once, you pink-faced pratt.

Is Jepcott pink-faced? Bapty has made him so, tinting and touching up the youthful executive's photograph with schoolboy glee until Jepcott looks little more than a schoolboy himself.

– Oh, by no means, Frank, Ralph, Rafe, I'm very much setting my cap at MetCable specifically at MetCable, which to my best belief which to my belief which so far as I'm concerned is the, has the, most exciting challenging has the most potential best potential offers all the excitement of getting in on the ground floor of a really stimulating challenging—

It's all rattling around in there somewhere. He'll wing it

21

when the moment comes. Tired of smart-arse Jepcott and his smart-arse trick questions, Bapty fancies a little escapism. He fades day into night, as with a dimmer-switch. Now it's this evening. The day would seem to have gone well, for he is enjoying a self-congratulatory brandy on the Pullman home – this despite the fact that the Portsea Belle has not run for a good ten years now. From his top pocket he produces a massive Havana cigar – given to him, it would seem, by a director of Metropolitan Cable at a hurriedly-arranged board-room reception to introduce Bapty to the top brass – and hands it to the youngish man sitting opposite him with the words:

– Here, you like these things. So do I, if it comes to that, but my doctor doesn't. Spherical objects.

Don't allow yourself to be confused here. That *spherical objects* was a mere aside to Dr Windows who, genie-like, momentarily materialised at this reference to him. It is how, although he does not know it, his patient dismisses his professional advice.

The man Bapty is addressing now, whose name appears to be Yellowley, is a sharp-featured sharp dresser with a smooth blue chin, who looks as if he could probably be a tax accountant. Unless he has need of him professionally, not at all Bapty's type, you probably wouldn't have imagined; yet here he is at his most unctuous, at his most oily you could even say, and feeling all warm and grateful from the fictitious euphoria of giving the man a make-believe cigar in a non-existent Pullman car.

You will come to see, as the day wears on, that Bapty has as great a need of a regular intake of sycophancy in his mental diet as a diabetic has of insulin. So many grammes of sucking-up *per diem* help balance the ravages of his temper.

In the act of lighting Yellowley's cigar from a flashy Met-Cable bookmatch, he is brought back to the present by the sight of one of his favourite scapegoats passing along the train – the real train, that is, not the Portsea Belle. It is the in-spector, checking tickets, even though that task has already been meticulously performed by the swining bloody-minded ticket collector at the barrier to platform four on Portsea station.

– You realise, I suppose, that the function you perform is so useless and unnecessary that it ought to be subject to ought to qualify for a grant as a job creation scheme? You do realise, of course, that you are contributing absolutely zero, either to the gross national product or the something services? Social services. Better word. Public services. Public good. You do realise, don't you, that I and all these other passengers are in effect carrying you on our backs?

Cutting and thrusting, phrasing and rephrasing, Bapty favours the inspector with the ingratiating half-smile intended by rights for Yellowley, and meekly displays his ticket as the train approaches East Croydon.

Time now for one of his standard texts. Who'd want to live in East Croydon? Why should anyone wish to be put to the trouble of being conceived, born, educated, apprenticed, employed, promoted, wooed, engaged, married and mortgaged, only to finish up in East poxy Croydon? He can do five minutes of this before getting to the inevitable bitter rider: Come to that, fancy ending up in Portsea. *At this dump*, as that cowbag used to say. But he's not ended up, not yet. The rest of your life starts tomorrow. Then the little surge of optimism sours to bile at once in Bapty's mouth, as he sees himself through the eyes of the smirking young man in the replica blue velvet suit, and by projection through the eyes of Ralph, Rafe, Jepcott. *And a three-time loser*, he adds for self-pitying good measure, referring to his marriages.

Looking for someone to hate he fixes on the nondescript woman standing out there on the platform, waiting for a local train. Nothing about her reminds him of Margot. Nothing sparks him off. He picks on her pettish frown and makes himself decide that she is so ugly she ought to be fined for it. Why does he glare at her so, his face pressed against the window, as the train moves off again? He is trying to project his monstrous opinion of her through the glass, willing her to

23

read his mind. She can't. Only you can do that. Don't let him catch you doing it, though, the fury he keeps getting into. He's a walking bomb these days, Bapty.

3

There's a blazing bungalow in his mind. He cannot have set fire to his home before leaving Marine Close this morning, otherwise you would have had feedback by now. This bungalow, he hypothesises, is on an estate in East poxy Croydon, and until Bapty drenched it in kerosene and put a match to it, was the property of the Buggerisation British Telecom sub-manager with responsibility for the state of the Victoria Station telephone booths.

– Sir: The first glimpse many foreign travellers have of London is of our Hall of Shame, Victoria Station . . .

Or better. Get the sod on Portsea Sound's Awkward Squad programme:

– So what you're saying is that our comments are biased and this figure of ninety-five per cent of payphones out of order is greatly exaggerated. All right. Now at this moment we have one hundred and thirty-eight volunteers voluntary observers stationed positioned standing by in each one of Portsea's one hundred and thirty-eight public phone booths, and on the stroke of nine they're all going to dial Portsea 8765 and try to get through to you here in the—

There is, if the truth be told, absolutely nothing wrong with the instrument Bapty is using. It is making all the correct noises as he dials, for all that he so much wishes it to be broken, to justify his arsonist intentions towards Buggerisation British Telecom, that he is maltreating the receiver almost to the point of vandalising it himself.

– So out of those three hundred and nineteen attempted calls, only nine have been able to get through. What do you say to that?

Luckily the phone booth is of the hooded type and so you are still privy to his thoughts. But you may not listen in to his conversation with Ruth. Stand clear.

This is not as straightforward as it at first seemed. He is thinking Ruth's telephone number but that is not what he is dialling. He is ringing Margot. As Bapty's reminiscing memory informs you, he does that occasionally – but only in his head. On past form, the phone he is using should not be so much vandalised as vaporised. It should not exist.

– I'd like to speak to Mrs Bapty, please. Mrs Margot Bapty. Yes you do have someone of that name, but she doesn't use it. Margot Shepherd. Your star writer, as she fancies herself to be. All right, then when she comes *back* from Birmingham Leeds Manchester, where you may depend on it she is screwing herself stupid with whoever she's supposed to be interviewing, just tell the little cowbag I rang, would you? Bapty. And the message is—

That's about as far as he takes it. He does have a message but it's so weak and lame – something on *she can get stuffed* lines: he really ought to polish it up a little – that always at this point he leapfrogs ahead in his mind and with an over-courteous *Gooood-bye*, in his mind hangs up.

He's not doing that today, he's only recognising that that's what he usually does. This time he's really dialled the number. Yet as he waits for the switchboard he's thinking *Ruth, Ruth*. Just her name. It recedes into a swirl of red mist as he begins to call up other names, descriptive of the swining pratt-faced pox-bollocking dozy pillocking telephone operator who is keeping him hanging on too long.

– Oh, there you are, switch. Not a public holiday after all. This is the chairman speaking. Before you connect me with my secretary would you be so kind as to explain why it's taken three and a half minutes to answer my—

He's got through. A lurch of panic as he realises he may be about to hear her voice. The phrase *Long time no see* offers itself for consideration, to be at once rejected, as is something about *Voice from the past*. His thought processes are very fuzzy in the stirred-up state he's got them into, but he's trying to rehearse what he'll say to her. It seems to have to do with taking her to lunch.

– Touch wood, I *may* have something to celebrate . . .

Ah, but supposing he hasn't? A pathetic reunion that'd be. She's already called him a lame duck more than once, as you may judge from the film-trailer excerpts from their stand-up rows which he briefly re-runs whenever memory jogs:

– Don't bugger about the bush, then. What you're trying to say is, I'm a failure.

– I wouldn't put it as crudely, or as cruelly as that, Sam. What I am trying to say is that if you're a success, I've just won the Woman of the Year award.

You may beg leave to doubt whether that was a genuine re-run – that particular exchange sounds too pat and polished to have really taken place. Nor has it: you can tell by his instant tidying-up of Margot's barb to read:

– If you're a success, ducky, I'm Woman of the Year.

She always has called him Sam, though. Somewhere among those memory clips there's one of her rubbing his nose into his middle-agedness by telling him that Edgar is such a middle-aged name. That's genuine, although his anthology of stinging rejoinders isn't.

All right, Bapty, try this:

– Oh, just up for the day, you know. I thought if you'd nothing on, if you'll pardon the expression—

Cut.

– Oh, just up for the day, you know, and being at a loose end over lunchtime—

Cut.

– Oh, just up for the day, you know . . .

A stab of disappointment. She's not in yet. Very unlikely that she would be at this hour, as he ought to know, yet his dismay is no less keen. That's the switchboard operator he's speaking to:

– Look, friend, I'm not asking for her size in French knickers. All I want is her direct line number. I'm doing you a favour, buggerlugs – next time I call I shan't have to drag you away from your crossword, shall I?

Evidently he has expressed himself more civilly than that, for he is scribbling down a number while simultaneously, by his expression, uttering an ingratiating word of thanks.

Meanwhile, from an adjoining chamber of Bapty's mind, a ponderous, measured voice intones, seemingly from the depths of a comfortable armchair:

– You see, old man, that's why the switchboard service is so sloppy. Anyone who's anyone in that organisation has a direct line, so the powers that be never realise how long it takes to—

Bapty, taking his stolid cue from this stolid observation, interjects droningly before the droning that prompts it has run its course:

– It's the same with London Transport, where all the executives ride about in official cars . . .

Despite being one of his regulars, the mental guest who attends to these words of wisdom with pipe-smoking, head-wagging approval, has no features to speak of, although he resembles Bapty himself in build and posture, and no fixed identity, apart from exuding the impression that he could be called Henry. By the cut of his check suit, he is an older man. Perhaps he is the ghost of Bapty's future. At any rate the exchange is so shamingly boring that Bapty brings it to an abrupt end by plugging himself back into the pang of disappointment he was experiencing at Margot's non-availability, and which he has yet to savour to the full.

The sweet pinprick of pain becomes a bayonet lunge as he wonders darkly where she might be, having rejected out of hand the mundane probability of her being at home finishing her breakfast. As practically always when he conjectures so – for whenever Bapty runs a mental spot-check on Margot's whereabouts, she is never where she is supposed to be – he finds her laid out like lamb and salad on a leather couch in a photographer's studio in a mews off Berkeley Square, wearing little but a ribbon around her neck and long black gloves, one arm trailing down to a tipped-up glass of champagne on the floor, her legs poised vertically as in the advertisement for stockings from which Bapty has borrowed freely for this lascivious reconstruction.

But at half-past nine in the morning? Well, why not? It was even earlier that first time, you may gather from Bapty's inner chunterings – the first time he has proof of, that is. She'd left the flat at just after nine, saying she wanted to stop off at Peter Jones on her way to the office. See him watching her from the bedroom window as she leaves the flat, too plump in her trim black suit then as he is too plump in his blue velvet suit now. You cannot see her face but you have the picture of one who eats too many chocolate liqueurs – an impression heightened by the untidy, cheaply-luxurious bedroom where Bapty stands, which with its scattered satins and deep red flock wallpaper is itself reminiscent of an empty chocolate box awash with plundered wrappers and still reeking of its guzzled contents.

Remembering himself at the window Bapty remembers how he watched her turn into Gloucester Road on her way to the tube station, then left the flat himself and took a cab to Sloane Square and waited across the road from the store by Lloyds Bank. She never went near Peter Jones that morning. If she did, why didn't she purchase anything, being notoriously incapable of walking through a shop door without spending money? If she did make a purchase, what became of it? The Peter Jones bag, the receipt, the affidavit of the assistant who served her? (Bapty sometimes does this as a court scene.)

He gave her an hour then rang the office. She was only a woman's page hack at that time and would be expected to leave a contact number where she could be reached. One of the fashion writers volunteered it, probably out of malice – Margot, or so Bapty has told himself, was unpopular with her female colleagues even before she became the prima donna he tells himself she is now.

He has that whole day stored as on a video-tape. Scene five, take one: Berkeley Square, noon. Long shot of Margot framed in a stone archway as she walks out of the cobbled mews and into the viewfinder of Bapty's memory, all aglow and fat-cat contented. Re-take: the same shot, but with a leather-jerkined figure in dark glasses waving her off from a varnished stable-type door with a Lamborghini parked hard by.

A successful sod, Bapty grudgingly concedes as he sits through the rushes, though circumstantial evidence can be marshalled, or manufactured, of his having become a bit of a has-been now. Bapty, now reviewing an enjoyable out-take of the once-celebrated photographer bumming drinks in a pub, lives in hopes of reading of his bankruptcy one of these fine days. Better: his prosecution as an undercover porn king. There is not even circumstantial evidence of this, not even the tiniest bubble of hearsay for Bapty to float as hard fact, but would it not just bring home to that cowbag the depths she has sunk to if only it were true?

(Note Bapty's tenses. He sometimes re-thinks old thoughts as freshly as if they were new ones.)

Bapty has never, either, set eyes on the nude photographs of Margot which he unearths from time to time in a variety of ingenious hiding places – sometimes the discovery involves his re-renting his old flat and prising up the floorboards – yet he knows they were taken. The cuckolding faggot is famous for that ploy. (Note now how Bapty half-wants to believe the heterosexual worst of Margot's 'little photographer friend' as he disparagingly thinks of him, pretending out of jealous spite to have difficulty in remembering his quite well-known name; yet also half-wants him to be a mincing semi-homosexual or near-eunuch, in comparison with whom Bapty himself is a rampant stud. The conflicting halves have long ago fused into this paradoxical whole.)

Bapty has noted, sieving the small print of a glossy magazine interview for veiled hints that the cuckolding faggot is known by those in the know to be secretly impotent, that the woman is yet to be born who will refuse to pose for him, and that the experience *turns them on* as he put it, or as Bapty now believes he put it while still acknowledging faintly that *some of them can get quite turned on* was nearer to it. Why should Margot

be the one exception, given her later track record? Bapty
knows, as surely as if he had seen it through a telescope, all that
went on that morning. A full transcript of the inquest remains
readily on file.

– Sam, I've told you and told you. I was there working. I was
selecting fashion pictures.

– To appear in the paper when?

– To appear in the paper never, because they didn't happen
to be what we wanted.

You still do not see her – they are both voices off or rather, as
on television, voices over, as Bapty's mental camera pans
across that silky, still unmade, whorish double bed. Perhaps it
is supposed to be symbolic of Margot, although it has to be
said that Bapty's mind does not go in much for symbolism.

– I can check all this, Margot, you know.

– You lift up that telephone, ducky, and I walk out of this
flat. Now I mean that, Sam.

– No need to panic, my dear, I wouldn't dream of embarrassing you.

– Piss off. What the hell's brought all this on, anyway?

– You said you were going to Peter Jones and then to the
office.

– I said I was going to Peter Jones and then to bloody work.
If I'd known you wanted a complete itinerary of my day's
movements, I would have made one out.

– Come on, Margot, you know what you were up to.

– If that's what you really, seriously think, and you're not
just bored and wanting to have a go, why don't we call it a day?

If it is truly what he thinks – whether or not that was a true
unexpurgated record of the interrogation as it took place, if it
did take place – then why should he wish to take her out to
lunch? There is, as you may judge from the soundings you are
able to take, no forgiveness in Bapty's heart, no time-softened
sentimental mellowing. Yet, and it is here to see, he has himself
waiting for her in heart-pounding anticipation at a plush
banquette for two in what is or perhaps was or is evidently
meant to be – he could very well have furnished it from the

31

scene-dock of his imagination – a favourite restaurant for both of them. It is odd.

All this has raced through Bapty's mind with flicker-book speed in the time it has taken to scribble down Margot's direct line number (that he does not have it already is a sure indication that they have not been in touch since they parted – worth remembering when Bapty's mind tries to suggest otherwise), profusely thank the operator while simultaneously booking him for an appearance on the Awkward Squad, and press down the receiver rest.

Ruth. As if working to an agenda he dismisses the fleshy, orchid-like abstract of the still unseen Margot and calls up the tranquil, solemn, intelligent oval face, framed by long straight hair, of a woman of about thirty in a high-necked dress, who gazes at him frankly and steadily as from a photograph. Perhaps it truly is a photograph: she does not speak or move. Now at last Bapty really is about to call her: he repeats her name to himself as he feels for change. *Ruth, Ruth*: he gives it a yearning quality, but one that is induced rather than infused: it gives him a small painful pleasure, like the squeezing of a spot. Ruth's photograph, if that's what it is, now smiles sadly, a dinner-party Mona Lisa.

He doesn't have the correct coins. A wisp of some previous diatribe on the elementary obviousness of the case for change machines floats away like an autumn leaf as he descends to the tube station, where he produces a pound note and buys a forty pence ticket. You must do the same if you are to keep track of him. Now equipped with a little stack of tenpenny pieces he looks towards the telephone booths. Two out of the six are unoccupied but there is a change-clinking throng around the other four, indicating that the vacant ones must be out of order. As a blazing roof-beam crashes to the ground, the Buggerisation British Telecom sub-manager rushes out of the inferno bent double, the clothes on his back alight.

4

You should not make assumptions – you nearly lost him there.

It is not the Victoria Line into the West End he is heading for but the District Line to South Kensington. He has other fish to fry before his Metropolitan Cable interview. *Spherical objects*, he responds automatically at the reminder from himself that his appointment with Dr Windows is in thirty-five minutes' time.

Scowling mentally at the ticket collector for uselessly lolling in his box while passengers struggling with suitcases have to process themselves through the automatic barriers, Bapty descends to platform one. He has it in for railway staff, Bapty does: they loom large in his mind. Passengers too, many of them. Looking around for, and to his pleasure locating, a bearded foreign-student type toting a back-pack, he projects him without further ado into a near-empty tube train with the back-pack taking up the one seat Bapty chooses to occupy. There is no altercation: the student sullenly failing to respond to a civil request to cease treating the seat as a luggage-rack, Bapty calmly flings the back-pack the length of the carriage, sits down and unfolds his newspaper.

This little playlet having satisfactorily run its course, he seeks further distraction, a row with a railway employee for preference. His mind running idle, the lit-up destination board indicating a Wimbledon train reminds him faintly and rather convolutedly – via Wimbledon's connection with tennis con-necting with the municipal courts up in Glassborough con-necting with his old flat backing on to them, all those years ago – of his first wife Pam. The pumpkin face of a beauty queen gone to seed – she was Miss Glassborough when they met, as you can see from the sash with which he nearly always adorns her – appears fleetingly and then is gone. You'll notice that he thinks very little about Pam these days. A passing, half-tolerant *silly bitch*, perhaps, as he remembers her empty-headed ways: but more often than not, any recollection of her is but a trigger to nostalgic memories of Glassborough's cramped little radio studios over a multiple tailor's – the only time, as Bapty always tells himself wistfully and as he tells himself now before ditching the subject, that he had any fun.

He can't think of his first wife, though, without giving a token thought to his second, June – Juney, as he still calls her – and their tiny semi in what passed in Glassborough for a residential suburb. (Not, he reflects peripherally, that a bungalow in Portsea is such a giant leap from those days.) The house figures as largely in this passing recollection as she does. Observe the ladder propped against the eaves. Should you come across a leaking roof in Bapty's mind, you may safely bet that he has either been reminded of Juney or is about to be. Leaking roofs, jobs about the house, the car needing servicing, anything of that kind suggesting domestic responsibilities, is liable to summon up Juney's petulant frown; while conversely he has only to think of Juney – even when she's trying to look seductive in her mail-order baby-doll nightie – to summon up a leaking roof. Will Margot, one day, remind him of anything so suburbanly mundane? It has become a matter of chortling pride to Bapty – a measure of his sophistication, he regards it as, or affects to regard it as – that the second of his three wives evokes only a bucket under a dripping ceiling. The truth is, though, as you may have divined from the abrupt shutting-off of her name as with a stopcock, that he goes all shifty at any surfacing of Juney. He'd rather not think of her at all, that's the size of it.

And in any case, he wants to think about his war with the railways. Sauntering up and down platform one, abstractedly nominating those waiting passengers most richly deserving of being pushed under the next train, he selects from many unfought battles the case of the British Rail clerk at Portsea

Station – a natural for the Awkward Squad slot, if ever he came across one – who once refused to lend the man ahead of Bapty in the ticket queue a pen with which to sign his credit card voucher.

Bapty has done a complete re-make of this incident, casting himself as the protagonist while considerably fleshing-out the part. The script, it has to be said, is rather confused. There are high managerial staff in evidence, as well as a platoon of railway police holding back the angry crowd of commuters who are unable to buy their tickets until the business has been sorted out, while two of their number, a sergeant and an inspector, take the clerk into custody. There is a railway by-law that Bapty knows about but the wretched clerk doesn't, whereby he is compelled on request to lend any prospective passenger his pen, which in any case happens to be BR property and so is not his to withhold in the first place. He is also to be charged with the theft of Bapty's Access card, which, on the basis of having already made out ticket and credit card voucher, he has been refusing to hand back until Bapty has acquired a pen and signed. To the British Rail and union officials attempting to persuade him to withdraw the charges in the interests of industrial peace, Bapty responds cordially:

– Gentlemen, it does not matter two shakes of a pig's behind to me if the whole of Southern Region shudders to a halt. Or, for that matter, the Eastern Region, the London Midland Region, the Western Region, the Scottish Region, Sealink, the Bluebell Line, Wagons-Lits, Canadian Pacific, the Atcheson, Topeka and Santa Fe . . .

So the time passes pleasantly enough for Bapty until his tube arrives to convey him, while briefly en route for South Ken, on a flying visit to his and Margot's old flat off Gloucester Road, which for all that it is one station further along the line than his corporeal journey will be taking him today, is customarily summoned up for him by various landmarks on this stretch of the District Railway.

There's that chocolate-box bedroom again. Either he must have spent a lot of time in it or he wishes he had. That's a nice big drawing room. Good antique furniture: there's the eighteen-something-or-other escritoire at which Margot proposed to make a start on her unwritten novel, and which he regularly used to ransack in search of love letters; the sideboard with its battery of decanters challenging him to become an alcoholic and teach her a lesson; the long mahogany dining table – Queen Anne when bought, early Victorian when sold – at which he believes he played host to at least two, possibly three, of Margot's lovers. It all had to go when they bought the bungalow. Bapty wonders where all that stuff is now. In a brief and fanciful fit of mawkishness, he sees the rest of his life at auction, failing to meet the reserve price.

From the steamy bathroom Margot calls:

– An hour and five minutes from Victoria, isn't it? You could commute.

– No I couldn't. The contract specifies living in Portsea.

– Then *I* could commute. From there to here.

– Yes, I can see you doing it. And how long before you missed the last train and had to stay in Town?

– So because you don't trust me I have to give up my career and bury myself up to the neck in shingle in a tinpot little seaside resort! What do you want me to do all day?

– Start your sexy romantic novel. You must have researched it thoroughly enough by now.

This doesn't sound like the kind of stuff that gets shouted through bathroom doorways – more like lines from a play. And indeed, the wet sponge that comes flying through the doorway in response to that last retort of Bapty's belongs more to light comedy than to real life. That is most probably the size of it: the scene Bapty had with Margot – and there must have been one – where he announced his decision to move to Portsea and take her with him, has become literally, theatrically rather, just that in his mind: a scene, all cut and dried and clean and sanitised, and kept on the level of banter. Adroitly, urbanely, Bapty marshals telling proof of his wife's infidelity – delivers ultimatums – Margot protests but capitulates. End of act one. As the curtain falls, though, you may hear behind it, if

36

you listen carefully, some mumbled, stumbled words of Bapty's about new leaves and fresh starts, and Margot's sighed agreement that anything is worth a try.

The play is over, abandoned during the interval. You re-discover Bapty still in the flat, unhappy and uneasy, but not at the prospect of continuing his big scene with Margot. She is no longer on the premises. You find him back in the living room, damp palms imprinting polished mahogany as he faces a bespectacled, foxy-looking individual – a dealer, evidently, at once cunning and poker-faced – across the Queen Anne/early Victorian dining table.

– I'm sure you're very well versed on antiques, very know-ledgeable about well up on antiques, Mr So and So, but your education I'm afraid your education has been sadly neglected sadly lacking, I'm afraid you know toss-all about furniture . . .

Oh dear. He must have made a bad bargain there. Like an embarrassed host, Bapty strives to change the subject as the tube decants him at South Ken station.

His expression is distant as he passes through the ticket barrier, barely registering the two chatterboxes it requires to man it. Something about *running the conversational gauntlet* makes itself felt, but it is a snatch from an encounter with a previous brace of ticket collectors – he is too busy to do the present pair justice now. They don't know how lucky they are.

Lips moving, brow furrowed, head cocked on one side, right hand executing little chopping motions like a dance-band conductor's, Bapty, as he moves hesitantly along the station forecourt, might be pacing his office while a stenographer takes dictation. He is.

– Dear Sir, I have been a resident of the Royal Borough a ratepayer in the Royal Borough for eleven years, residing throughout the whole nearly all of that period at the above address, and driving company cars provided for my exclusive use by my employers Thames Radio Ltd. It should therefore be well established by now that (a) I am a bona fide resident, (b) I am in possession of a car, and (c) by virtue of (a) and (b) I am entitled to a resident's parking permit under the Kensington and Chelsea (Parking Places) Order 1967. May I ask therefore may I ask why therefore may I therefore ask why on each and every occasion when this permit has to be renewed, you persist in requiring renewed, fresh, renewed, every occasion on which this permit is due for renewal, you insist on persist in requiring proof of residency and permit entitlement . . .

It is perhaps his favourite letter of all time, and one which he actually sent. Not, it has to be said, in anything like its present form, for it has been reworked many times during perambulations through this area. Every visit to Dr Windows adds a new improvement – a sardonic touch here, an ironic twist there. The traffic wardens must wonder why a middle-aged pedestrian scowls at them so, little realising their surrogate role as swining piss-balling jumped-up little penpushers in the parking control office and participants in a new spin-off from Portsea Sound's Awkward Squad programme, called Face The Public.

Nor can they realise, as he turns into this narrow thoroughfare of boutiques and restaurants, still sporting its sign NO VEHICULAR ACCESS TO CROMWELL ROAD despite all Bapty's satirical unposted letters to *The Times* and other journals about its pedantry, that he is a pedestrian no longer but the driver of that coal lorry which is jamming the street, having been stopped by a policeman.

– Can you read, sunshine?

– Not only can I read, officer, but I can also write, and shall be doing so this very evening to your superior, Chief Superintendent So and So, laying a formal complaint against your grossly offensive manner towards a member of the public.

So mightily pleased at the fluency of this retort that his inward smile of satisfaction plays visibly on his twitching lips, Bapty enters Mr Trim, hairdressing boutique.

Though empty of clients at this early hour, the L-shaped salon with its egg-blue quilted walls and gently-wafting classical music has a positively unisex air – not Bapty's style at all, you wouldn't have thought. The reply *Fine, Tony, fine* poised in readiness for the unasked question *How's madame?*

from the young manager who has detached himself from the knot of chattering crimpers and advanced to greet him, suggests that possibly Margot put him on to the place when they lived around here.

Yes – it's at once evident that she did:

– I must look like a poofter.

– You look very smart, provided you don't comb it out again. Off you go, then, and good luck. Ring me and tell me how it went.

Margot, plucking hairs from his lapels, seems to be sending him off about his interview with Metropolitan Cable today. He must have reconstructed this material from a recollection of her sending him off about his interview with Portsea Sound three years ago – or is it a recollection of how he hoped and even longed to be sent off, when in the event she left the flat for the day without even remembering where he was going? A roller-coaster heave of self-pity tells you that that is the way it was.

Appointment Not Always Necessary, says the sign. That makes it all the easier for you to occupy one of the row of chairs around the corner of the L, well out of Bapty's way, where you may comfortably listen to what he has to say to himself additional to *Can't you find that pack of nancy boys something to do, Tony? They create a very bad impression, you know*, the observation that crosses his mind as he is led to his own chair.

This will surprise you. As Tony begins his barber's prattle – something about the Common Market and French apples, from the fragments Bapty allows to infiltrate his consciousness – you are expecting an exasperated reaction. *What the fuck do you know about the Common Market?* perhaps, or *Look, my friend, I've come in here for a haircut, not a lecture on pigging agriculture.* But though both these rejoinders line up to be thought, applying so to speak to be given formal shape, they are at once suppressed like words unspoken. Instead:

– Franchising, that's what you're talking about, Tony.

– That's it exactly, Mr Bapty. Like McDonald's. Only these

would be more your old-fashioned barbershops, complete with shoe-shine stand, cigar counter, blonde manicurist, the lot.

– Not forgetting your barber's pole at the correct angle, Tony.

– Oh, definitely, got to have the old barber's pole. So you think it's a good idea, Mr Bapty?

– I think it's a bloody marvellous idea. Have you costed it?

Tony begins to spout figures but Bapty doesn't heed them. He isn't even here any more. He's at lunch. The Captain's Table, the flashy fish restaurant in Portsea, by the look of it. The barber's towel round his neck has become a lobster bib.

– So you'd call it a good investment?

– It's more than a good investment, Edgar, it's such a first-rate business opportunity I think you ought to raise your own capital and float the franchise yourself. Both here and in America.

You recognise Bapty's financial adviser in the shiny shark-skin suit. It is Yellowley, the recipient of that free cigar on the Pullman back to Portsea tonight. Getting Yellowley's approval on business matters seems important to Bapty. He is as pleased at having brought him a sound investment idea as a cat at bringing home a mouse. But he does, over the strawberry shortcake, experience a flicker of unease.

– What about Tony, though?

– What about him?

– His idea.

– No copyright in ideas, chum.

Hating his barber for compromising him so, Bapty knocks back his brandy and swings viciously back to the salon where, all unknowing of the plot that has just been hatched to swindle him out of a fortune, Tony snips complacently away at his client's datishly trendy sideburns.

– I shan't be coming here again, Tony, by the way. No, it's been nice knowing you and all that but in fact in future I'll be going in future I'll be using in fact I'm switching my allegiance to the gents' hairdressing salon in the underground bog at

Portsea Station. He cuts hair like a one-armed gardener mowing a lawn but he does happen to be he does have the advantage of being he does have one outstanding asset. He's not a raging poofter.

Much as he has enjoyed this interlude with Tony, Bapty is tired of the game now. Even as he mentally shapes this last sally he is allowing it to balloon off over the horizon as weightier matters demand his attention.

Wrinkled spherical objects, observes Bapty, addressing his medical adviser.

5

— Since in fact we now have in fact since in fact a precedent has been arrived at whereby since in fact a precedent has been established whereby you have accepted a photostat of the registration document without further unnecessary documentary without further unnecessary proof that I am the sole user of the vehicle in question, perhaps you would tell me, in the event of my being refused a parking permit by virtue of not producing the documents not complying with the procedure you have since laid down, on what basis you might propose to prosecute me under the Kensington and Chelsea (Parking Places) Order 1967 for non-possession of a permit; furthermore—

It is no good. As a rule, the letter rambles effortlessly along all the way to Dr Windows' surgery in Old Brompton Road: sometimes, indeed, he is obliged to hover on the doorstep in order to get it completed and signed – . . . *shall be forwarding copies of this correspondence to my solicitors, Messrs Windows and, oh, Yellowley* – before pressing the entry-phone button. This morning, as he is wafted along in a haze of cologne and hair conditioner, self-consciously sauntering in order both to use up the six minutes still to spare before his appointment and to slow down his racing heart, his own voice drives his own voice out:

— I was in fact boy scout's honour down to eleven stone eight eleven three eleven five a few weeks ago, Doc, but as luck would have it I've been caught up in such a welter of business lunches lately—

Will he try that one on?. Something like it, probably. He

either usually does or usually means to, by the practised, even hackneyed, ring of that excuse.

– Oh dear oh dear oh dear oh dear oh dear. One sixty over ninety. Now that's not good enough, Mr Bapty, as you very well know.

– No.

Or to put it another way:

– Wrinkled spherical objects.

His blood pressure count, seemingly. That must be what the doctor said to him the last time. Or the time before. Or what he anticipates him saying this time. Bapty's mental diary shows that he comes up every three months for this check-up – six months it used to be – and with every visit gets a warning.

– Had to come up anyway to see my quack. Oh, nothing serious. Good excuse for a day out, frankly: see a few old mates, catch up on the gossip.

That's to Ralph Jepcott. On reflection – second thoughts constantly shadow his first thoughts, and third thoughts his second – he promptly eliminates it from the cud of half-digested conversational scraps he may or may not regurgitate at that MetCable interview later on. It will not do to present himself as a skiving semi-invalid. Bapty sweats through his lavishly-applied Mr Trim after-shave at having prospectively put himself in such a bad light, then allows himself to feel, in passing, hard done-by at his mind's knack of so putting a boomerang-spin on a remark that has never been delivered and is now unlikely to be, that he nevertheless experiences the same retrospective embarrassment as if it had been. Bapty does not perhaps appreciate that his mind has just done him a great favour, equivalent to the service performed for vertigo sufferers by the nervous compulsion to jump.

– One eighty over h'm. No, that's not at all good news, is it, Doc? Without making excuses, though, do bear in mind I do happen to be do take into consideration I do have to say in my own defence it would be rather strange if I weren't a bit tensed up today of all days, bearing in mind I have a very ticklish job interview coming up.

This appears to cut little ice with Dr Windows who is going on about salt consumption and urine tests as Bapty reaches the area railings of the stucco terrace housing his surgery. Walking slowly already, he slows down to a dawdle to calm himself. A white-faced, punkishly-inclined youth in baggy black clothes like a harlequin in mourning, humping an ear-blasting radio in a plastic tote-bag, approaches from the opposite direction along what Bapty chooses to believe is his own territorial strip of pavement. Seizing the radio and hurtling it to land in smithereens in Dr Windows' area basement, Bapty sticks remorselessly on his pre-set course, determined not to give way. The youth, however, obligingly sidesteps to the middle of the pavement several paces earlier than is necessary to avert a collision, yet only fractionally before Bapty reaches the man-hole cover which, in truth, marks the pre-ordained point at which he himself would have given way. The placatory gesture will not save the unfortunate youth. Holding his ground, Bapty barges into his shoulder with such force that he is sent reeling into the gutter. A kick in the ribs and another in the groin, then Bapty grinds his heel in the blaring radio which seems to be back in its owner's possession, reducing it once more to scrap before panting triumphantly up Dr Windows' steps and pressing the entryphone buzzer to be admitted for his blood-pressure test.

The waiting room is large enough for you to sit at the far end of it without troubling Bapty, who in any event would seem to have nothing to say to the receptionist beyond mumbling his name. Except for routinely recording *mole on neck*, he hardly spares her a thought: surprising that – she is attractive enough to have become his past or future mistress in the time he has been coming here; either that, or to have incurred his dis-pleasure in some way, so qualifying, perhaps, for one of the poison-pen letters he occasionally composes when time hangs heavily.

The receptionist will not notice you unless you should manifest yourself outside the mind of Bapty. Bapty himself will not be aware that he is playing hermit crab to your presence unless, by intrusion into his everyday affairs, you draw attention to yourself. The reminder may not be necessary but it is as well to be on the safe side.

Bapty picks up a discarded *Daily Telegraph* and scans the headlines, but so perfunctorily that only a garbled transmission of half a dozen words – POLITE IN BOTTLES, DARLING FISHERMEN and CALF RECLUSE – reaches his retina before he listlessly turns the pages, taking nothing in, while at the same time paradoxically reproaching himself for not buying a paper at Portsea Station this morning and keeping up with the news. As Bapty ploddingly confides to Henry, the solid, faceless citizen in the check suit who has come to enjoy a pipe with him under the Thank You For Not Smoking sign, he cancelled the newspapers on the very day Margot left, since not only the rag she was re-joining but all the other rags remind him of the cowbag.

His audience is bovinely sympathetic, as comforting as a baby's dummy.

– Best way, old man. I know when Phillipa died, I became allergic to marmalade. It had always been one of our standing jokes, you see – well, I say standing joke, it was more of a standing feud. Every morning after breakfast we'd swop newspapers and lo and behold if I didn't invariably find her *Guardian* smeared with marmalade. Infuriating.

Bapty, recognising this little reminiscence as his own property, in respect of his first wife Pam – although her paper was not the *Guardian* but the *Daily Express*, and it wasn't marmalade but jam and butter that she got all over it – explodes *Is this a newspaper or a pigging sandwich? Why don't you shove it in the toaster and be done with it?* by way of dismissing all this nonsense from his mind. He wants a word with Ralph Jepcott.

– As a matter of fact, Ralph, I don't read the newspapers as a matter of in point of fact, Rafe, I don't read the newspapers as a matter of policy. If Portsea Sound isn't keeping me properly abreast with the news, then there's something seriously wrong with our service and it's up to me to get something up to me to do something up to me to something something something, a

45

serious flaw in our service and it's up to me to get something done about to get the situation remedied.

— I buy that, Edgar, but let me ask you this. If you don't read the papers, how do you know what you're competing against?

— Good question.

Not caring to dip into the collage of words and phrases from which he might have selected his answer, for fear that there is nothing really in there except gibberish, Bapty considers the three other patients in the waiting room, his eye gliding over the empty chair in which you unobtrusively sit.

As you can see, they are a nondescript bunch: not a face or a feature he, or you, will remember for a second after their departure: yet when there is next a walk-on part in one of the little dramas he plays to himself — a waiter, a customer in the post office, a fellow-passenger on the bus where he is having a row with the swining bollock-kneed Herpes-carrying conductor — look closely, and you may see that it is one of these three. It is in idle moments among anonymous company such as this that Bapty, all unknowingly, casts his extras.

With a sudden lifting of the spirits, Bapty congratulates himself, as he half-focuses on that depressed-looking grey-faced clerical type of about his own age who probably has something dreadfully wrong with him, on not being any of these people. How awful it must be for them to be them: how, he wonders, warming to his theme, can any of them bear not to be Bapty, given the evidence before their eyes of what he is compared with what they are? When Bapty next tells himself (so he tells himself) that he is not much of a catch, he will think back on these three and revise his estimation of himself in an upward direction.

— Whereupon I promptly revised my opinion of myself in an upward direction!

Laughter. Applause. The denouement goes down well at the unspecified annual dinner where Bapty is the main speaker. He must find an anecdote to fit it.

Sitting on either side of the grey-faced man, a *cordon sanitaire* of empty chairs between them, two colourless women

46

– of uncertain age, Bapty recounts with twinkling pedantry, stocking his non-existent anecdote with them – make up the trio of patients. So pronounced is their colourlessness, at any rate to Bapty, that it is their main feature, and so similar a feature that they might be twins. The grey-faced man looks florid by comparison, notes Bapty – who then reflects that by comparison with the three of them, he himself must look like a walking beetroot.

Sod them. That, he impetuously, dismissively concludes, is what East poxy Croydon is for: to accommodate them and their like. He has been misguided to wonder how anyone can bear to live in East Croydon – they can bear it because they are the kind of people who live there.

Bapty feels smirkingly that he has thought something clever, but that it can be improved upon. He tries to sharpen his aphorism but it at once atomises into a swirl of infinite permutations of or variations upon itself – *kind of people who belong East Croydon type of person bear it only because East Croydon belong kind of people* . . . You will, Bapty, you will. He'll come back to it when his mind is less unsettled by the preoccupations of a tense and busy day. However, his relief upon having made that decision is tempered, as always when temporarily abandoning a half-baked epigram for ever, by a spasm of unease at his inability to discipline his thought processes. Is it anything to do with his health?

Cancer of the jaw, diagnoses Bapty as the grey-faced man is buzzed into the surgery. He shudders inwardly, compulsively touching his own jaw and experiencing a responsive, psychosomatic twinge. It has always been the worst disease Bapty can bring to mind – his secret fear, you might say, his Room 101. To be rid of it he tries to select new thoughts as if pressing the buttons of a radio. Ruth. Metropolitan Cable. Margot lunch. Yellowley. No good. By now half his face has been cut away. He oscillates through a scramble of word-static – *packing case, bramble, luggage bath, headway, seeds, knacker, farways, Brockenhurst* – until he is sufficiently distanced from his cancer operation to be able to tune in free of interference.

– This to be kept under your metaphorical hat and entered in your diary only if you have access to invisible ink. Leaving thrash – Winnie's Bar – last Friday of the month. Mine. No, I can't tell you where just yet but it's something I've been angling for. I'm very pleased. That's the bad news. The good news is that I just want you to know I'll be recommending you as my successor.

The recipient of these confidences is identified as one Oliver Pease, Bapty's assistant at Portsea Sound. Bright enough looking lad, lively face, well-groomed blond hair, carefully-casual or casually-careful in denim, but little more than the office boy, really, as Bapty, on some other wavelength, scornfully acknowledges. Only twenty-two years old, far too young to be Bapty's, or anyone else's successor, in management that is. Not that he has any wish to be: his ambition is to get in on the creative side – DJ, preferably. Bapty knows all this – *DJ my belly-button, you haven't got the voice, you haven't got the personality and you haven't got the gift of the gab*, you can hear his faint, crackling voice declaiming under his own words, as on a superimposed tape – yet he persists in hosting this dinner at the Captain's Table (his second meal there in half an hour: no wonder he's so gross) at which he gives Oliver the glad tidings, amending and improving as he goes along.

– That's the good news. The bad news is that I'm recommending you as my . . .

It pleases him, gives him a warm glow, makes him feel good. And at no cost.

– He's young, yes, but what he lacks in experience he gains, not gains, makes up for, in enthusiasm. And he knows what a young audience wants without having to spend half the budget on market research . . .

Bapty's addressing the Portsea Sound board of directors now, and very persuasive he is too. It is all the more curious since he has every reason to believe, or believes he has every reason to believe, that Oliver was seduced by Margot in his first month at the studios, when he was not yet twenty. A quick moonlit vignette of the boy alighting from a mini-cab in the

48

empty, sleeping Victorian crescent of converted flats and bed-sitters where he evidently lives: he must have been with her, for why else would the League of Justice be standing in wait in the shadow of the trees? – then Bapty whisks him into the otherwise deserted Winnie's Bar where they are to meet for a quick morning drink. Bapty witnesses himself enter.

– I've just left the top brass. There's only one thing I'm allowed to tell you, young man. The first is that you owe me a very large drink. The second is that you owe me another very large drink.

The pleasing indulgence occupies him until he is called into the surgery. There he goes now. Read the *Daily Telegraph*, Bapty shouldn't be long. You'll see that POLITE IN BOTTLES was POLICE IN BATTLES, DARLING FISHERMEN was DARING FISHERMEN and CALF RECLUSE was GALE RESCUES.

6

— One ninety over my left testicle. If I suffer from stress it's because I'm in a stressful job. Calm me down and you'll calm me straight into the bankruptcy court.

Not a word of this has passed his lips, of course. He rages along the Old Brompton Road, going the wrong way, having cleaved his mind into a split screen like a phone-call sequence in a TV sitcom. In one segment, while the inflatable cuff clamped to his throbbing arm transmits alarming, lie-detector signals to the sphygmomanometer, he is storming at Dr Windows about his need for stress. In the other, pacing his office in shirt sleeves, tie loose, one telephone cradled on his shoulder while he answers a second and a third shrills persistently, he invents the stress for which he claims the need. Or rather, he re-patents it, for the invention is not new, as you may detect from the closely-hatched, meticulously filled-in detail — the strewn papers, the congealed plates indicating a working lunch, the doodle-covered scratch pad, and so on. Bapty has put a lot of work into this tableau. He has probably even convinced himself by now, as he seeks by wish-telepathy to convince others, that it is taken from life.

Even Bapty must have a day off occasionally. Here he is on the golf-course with that flashy young man Yellowley. The conversation is to do with his share option at Metropolitan Cable. He tees off. His radio-pager bleeps.

Does Bapty carry a radio-pager? You already have reason to doubt his claim to membership of the Portsea Golf Club. Does he play golf even, would you say?

Dr Windows summons him back to earth, or at least coaxes him towards his flight path through the clouds.

– I appreciate that, Mr Bapty, I appreciate that. The Good Lord gave each and every one of us a task in life. Yours is to do your level best to kill yourself and mine is to prevent you from so doing by advising you to slow down. Now I'm not asking you to become a dormouse. Just don't go about your daily round like a bull in a china shop. Let your highly-paid staff take some of the strain.

Despite the fluency of this piece of reportage, it is unlikely that Dr Windows said anything remotely on those lines, although it may very well be a skilfully cut-together montage of past warnings. Bapty will not permit himself to hear what the doctor had to say to him this time round. *Bulldoze. Lamprey. Catnip. Parsons. Luggage bath.* It will trickle through in the end, though, like filtered coffee. You will just have to wait.

– All right, Doc, just tell me what you want me to do. Spell it out. Apart from keep taking the tablets.

– I do want you to keep taking the tablets, in fact I'm about to put you on a stronger dosage, but I'd be much much happier if only I could take you off them. Now I have to say this to you, Mr Bapty – it's a dangerous course you're on, believe you me.

– Spherical objects.

You know that Bapty doesn't talk to his doctor like that; but there is almost certainly something buried away in that exchange that was actually said. The ice formation around his heart is the giveaway.

See if you can separate the wheat from the chaff. No need: here it is. *A dangerous course you're on.* The phrase ricochets around his skull before he flings it boomeranging into what he hopes is oblivion but knows is not. Bapty is a frightened man.

– May I ask why, therefore, on each and every occasion when this parking permit has to be renewed, you persist in requiring renewed fresh repetition of duplicate documentary evidence that I am the sole user and keeper of the car vehicle in question?

He really is rattled. Usually, on these visits, the parking

permit letter gets only one reading. Yet here he is, repeating it like a mantra.

In desperation he equips his fictional stenographer with black stockings and has her cross her legs. But still he cannot stop the truth drip-dripping through the filter.

— Solemn warning . . . man of your weight, age and temperament . . . increasing workload on the heart muscles, d'ye follow me?

— Spherical objects.

Bapty is in bad shape and knows it, but doesn't want to know it.

— It is possible that you do not appreciate the amount of unnecessary office work caused entailed in raising this unnecessary in raising this unneeded completely superfluous documentation. In the first place, a memo has to be sent by me to my managing director. Normally such a routine matter would be a matter normally such a routine request would be a matter for my own office, but you have indicated that a letter with myself as signatory would be unacceptable to your squinting cross-eyed syphilitic piss-boiling good selves. . . .

In his panic the words flow almost effortlessly, their spate unchecked. It is a closely-typed, two-page letter on standard A4 usually, when brought to him for signature. The state he's in, it could come out at three or four foolscap pages.

— More than a question of diet, Mr Bapty . . . whole lifestyle . . . now you must bear with me while I speak frankly . . .

A welcome diversion for Bapty here, as he makes a citizen's arrest under the Litter Act, prompted by a dropped chocolate-bar wrapper. That the culprit cannot be more than four years old cuts no ice with him. It is her third offence. Bapty has her carried kicking and screaming out of the dock to begin a stiff Borstal sentence before he brings his mind back to the avoidance of Dr Windows.

— My managing director's secretary then has to locate in her files a copy copies of the letters sent despatched to the Parking Permit office in previous years, taking time off from her pressing duties to type an exact duplicate of it them the same, and place it before her employer for signature . . .

He cannot keep it up, he is too worried and upset. Profoundly troubled by what he has just done, he has the hysterical child brought back into court. Two policewomen comfort her, one of them making the mistake of offering her a chocolate bar of the very same brand that has brought her to her present predicament. The blotched, tear-soaked face crumples with terror at sight of the wrapper. Good. She has learned her lesson. The magistrate, kindly now, addresses her. He is Dr Windows.

– It's to be hoped that this salutary experience has been a lesson to you. Now I want you to go home and tell Mummy what you can both expect should you appear before me again. It's as much for my own good as for yours, Mr Bapty – losing patients is bad for my reputation, d'ye see . . .

Livid at his doctor for having sneaked in by the back door so to speak, Bapty's mouth shapes convulsively into a snarl as he almost spits his interjection out loud:

– Ah, wrinkled spherical objects!

– Can't cut your drinking down drastically, then do the sensible thing and cut it out altogether . . . every occasional cigar is an occasion too many . . . Now I mean what I'm saying to you, every word . . . Not merely your health we're talking about any longer, it's your survival . . .

Ashamed of his last outburst, fearful that passers-by will take him for one of those demented souls who stand in the middle of the road shouting or directing traffic, Bapty is suave now:

– Spherical objects of a prune-like consistency.

– Higher the blood pressure, the greater the chance of coronary heart disease. Now that's not kidology . . .

One moment. Bapty still has some unfinished business in connection with that wretched dropped chocolate wrapper. He is no longer glad of the diversion – would be gladder to be shot of it. The matter truly bothers him.

– What it has to do with me, madam, is that I happen to be a ratepayer. Every time your child drops a piece of paper, the Royal Borough of Kensington and Chelsea has to pay someone to pick it up. Now I don't know how well you know the law . . .

He has felt compelled to re-work the whole sorry episode, no longer having the child bundled into a police van to the astonishment of onlookers, but confining himself to a tap on the mother's shoulder and a none-too-friendly caution.

At peace now, he allows his guard to slip. Dr Windows seizes his opportunity:

– Like to reach the ripe old age of sixty, I imagine?

– Hairy, wrinkled, apricot-sized spherical objects. The letter then has to be channelled back to me, attached to my parking permit application and other documentation documents, and posted to you by me for processing by your pig-pissing legions of swining shitbagging snot-gobbling pox-bollocking—

– Heading for disaster, I do assure you . . .

Sporran. Woodcut. Pinpoint. Hemp. Luggage bath. Tarboil. Windsurf. Pamper. Netherwell.

– Now do be guided by me, Mr Bapty. And I shall want to see you not in three months but in one month. In fact better make that two weeks from today, and come prepared to go into hospital if need be.

– *There is a tavern in the town, in the town, where-here my true love sits him down, sits him dow-how-how-hown* . . .

If Bapty is singing in his head, it must be serious.

7

— Oh, it's absolute crap, old boy. You see, bear in mind these quacks have to play it by the book, but what you know and I know is that what's high for one individual isn't necessarily high for the next. It's all to do with your metabolism. You see, it's like drunken driving. Now if I'd been stopped on the way home last night, I'm pretty sure I should have turned their breathalyser all the colours in the rainbow, but I know perfectly well I was driving competently and carefully. Whereas someone else might have hardly a drop, and . . .

Bored into comparative calmness by his saloon bar alter ego Henry, Bapty realises at last that he is walking away from South Ken station, and that this must therefore be the corner of Gloucester Road.

— Sir, A stranger to the capital walking along Old Brompton Road in search of Gloucester Road would look in vain, for nowhere does the Royal Borough give the game away. Standardised, legible street-signs—

He makes a decision to continue in the direction he has taken, having first looked at his watch and registered *Twelve minutes*. That can hardly mean twelve minutes to his appointment at MetCable, otherwise he would be cutting it fine. On the contrary, he has time to kill: that much becomes evident as he pauses at the corner and breathes heavily in and out. He is trying to slow down by literally slowing down.

In fact better make that two weeks from today, and come prepared to go into hospital, Dr Windows is reiterating. To which Bapty makes a reply of such revoltingly scatological obscenity that he shocks not only you, if you were listening, but himself.

Charging up Gloucester Road, lips twitching as he thinks would-be tranquillising thoughts of a chug-chugging steam-train journey along the winding Cornish coast on a long-ago golden afternoon (selecting this from a small stock of peaceful memories, he has also remembered, or invented, a total of no fewer than five officious ticket inspectors who infest the train between Paddington and Penzance), he turns presently into Colchester Place where he lived with Margot before the move to Portsea.

Now this is quite interesting. Here is Colchester Place Mansions which he registers at once as his former home – the fourth floor flat there with the corner window below a slated turret. Yet although you know it was from that window that he watched Margot heading for Gloucester Road tube station on that morning of her alleged assignation in the mews off Berkeley Square, it does not in any way match the grand block of custom-built, renovated Edwardian flats which you saw in his mental footage as, with a change of shot, he had Margot stepping out of a gilded-cage lift and clacking across black and white tiles to the varnished double doors. That – you may have noticed the porter polishing its brass plate as you passed by a moment ago – was Viceroy Court, in Gloucester Road itself. Bapty has never lived there. It is where he would like to live, if he gets that MetCable job: and therefore he thinks of the flat he wants as the flat he had.

Colchester Place Mansions is an altogether more modest establishment – no more than a converted house really, despite its grandiose title, and run-down at that. It could have come down in the world since Bapty's time here, of course. It has. Before your eyes, the rotting window sills are newly plastered and painted, the chipped steps restored, the broken area railings replaced. Very smart it is, now. It is like one of those films where the fancy-framed sepia photograph of a seedy old clapboard house suddenly bursts into colour with the passing horse and buggie animated into clip-clopping life and the house all white and spanking new and filled with happy cries.

Or does Bapty exaggerate? That elegant drawing room of

his – was that all he has cracked it up to be? Yes, it does seem so. All the good stuff has gone to auction but you can see the proportions of the room through his eyes, and take in the pale Regency-striped panels and the high moulded ceiling, where for a moment a chandelier twinkles and then is gone. There are dust sheets everywhere and removal men are packing books into tea chests. One of them pauses to light a cigarette. Before he has even got the packet open, Bapty is on the dismantled telephone:

– Yes, I understood you would be sending three men in order that we might get ourselves settled in in, established in Portsea before nightfall. I believe three men is what in fact I'm being asked to pay for in your estimate. Now in fact what you have now what you have in fact sent me is, are, is, in fact you have sent me two workmen and one wanker. I think you should know that in the event of the Portsea house being unfit for us to sleep in tonight, we shall be taking up residence at the Majestic Hotel and sending you the bill . . .

Mental flashbacks are like cinematic ones: there is not necessarily any chronological sense to them. Standing outside his old flat, Bapty sees himself humping a blue suitcase up the steps after a holiday, but he cannot for the life of him remember which holiday. Cornwall comes into view again: rocks, a beach, a rambling clifftop hotel, but that was a childhood holiday it seems, certainly not one he took with Margot. Here he is now in Venice, gazing across the lagoon from the stern of a vaporetto. Paris: establishing shot of the Eiffel Tower. An island, Greek by the look of its peasant dance. Italy again: a flower market. Picture postcards of four honeymoons – yet he's only been married three times. One of them, the Greek island probably, hasn't taken place yet and perhaps never will. Ruth, with her solemn oval face so far in the back of his mind as to be but postage-stamp size, smiles her sad smile.

Resuming his arrival back at the flat from wherever he's been with the blue suitcase, he calls to mind the name of the people who nearly bought the lease – Verne – but can't recall the couple who did buy it in the end. Leapman, was it? No,

Lakeman. He knows very well that it wasn't, but decides impatiently that it might as well be, for there are other names waiting to be thought. Pugh. Garforth or Garford. Lawes. Respectively, two of the other flat owners and the estate agent who handled the sale. Mrs Calloway, the cleaning woman. A Polish name, all Zs and Ws, the caretaker. Iris, Mrs Calloway's first name. Bapty is keeping Dr Windows out of his head by every device he can.

He turns back towards Gloucester Road just as the disorienting ululation of a siren fills the air, swathing a path through the traffic for the ambulance that speeds Bapty to St Stephen's Hospital where he had his hernia operation. That it turns out to be a police car siren does not affect the scenario. Ruth, still in her Greek island honeymoon outfit, is by his bedside, sadly smiling. The tube up his nostril causes discomfort rather than pain. Is he about to make a death-bed speech? He toys with the notion, but the spectre of Dr Windows and his grim, told-you-so nod decides him to abandon it, and indeed instantly to discharge himself from the intensive care unit. Here he comes now, out through the gates, carrying that blue suitcase again and remembering at last where he had been with it. Not on holiday at all but to hospital: yet for all that he wasn't supposed to carry anything after his hernia operation, the cowbag wasn't there to take him home, being otherwise engaged performing fellatio upon an Italian fabrics designer while attending his fictitious press show at the Royal International Hotel. The lack of any persuasive corroborative detail, such as the subsequent castration of the Italian at the hands of the League of Justice, would suggest that Bapty doesn't really believe this account of Margot's absence. In fact the fashion page cutting he now turns up, as in a scrapbook, confirms that she was telling the truth and the press show was genuine. It does not stand in the way of his feeling suicidally badly done by as he trudges the blue suitcase homewards. Happily for Bapty's hernia, you saw the hospital porter helping him into a taxi.

Bureau de change, cambio, Wechsel. Jewellery antiques &

gifts. Shoe repairs. 2-hr de luxe dry cleaning. Photocopying. Stationery cards paperbacks. Continuing along Gloucester Road after his diversion to Colchester Place and Cornwall, he catalogues the shop signs as he goes. Some of them he physically sees, some he anticipates; others, newcomers since his day, he replaces with their original names – where you see Fastburgers he sees Pizza Palace, Keys Cut he substitutes with Heel Bar. The exercise is of no interest to either of you but it does keep Dr Windows at bay.

For once, at the anticipated sight of his old local, the Marquis of Granby, he has a proper, unfragmented memory: how, when they first came to live around here, not yet in Colchester Place but in some hazily-suggested, bohemian-seeming but probably romanticised attic flat not far away, he and Margot used to divide the Saturday morning shopping between them, taking one side of the road each, then meet up in the pub.

There he sits, a younger man then naturally – younger-looking now, probably, than he actually was at the time – with his string bags of oranges and vegetables, Chianti, Scotch and groceries at his feet, cutting quite a dash in his denims which he could carry off then, though he thinks it as shouldn't, with a packet of Disque Bleu and two schooners of sherry on the brass-rimmed table in his and Margot's regular corner.

Henry is there at the bar with a pewter tankard, called into being in error by the saloon bar aura of Bapty's reverie.

– Same as me, old boy. Forty a day I was on – gave it up just like that.

Bapty doesn't want to discuss the subject. He is beginning to crave the cigar he knows he mustn't have. *Luggage bath*, he observes curtly to Henry; and to Henry's companion, *Spherical objects*. Ignored, the intruders will go away soon.

He rises, stubbing out his Gauloise and folding up his *Guardian* – her *Guardian*, more accurately – as, simulating exhaustion, she makes her jokey knee-buckling entrance in a flurry of baguettes, butcher's parcels, magazines and raffia-tied pastrycook's cartons. He takes her duffel coat. She's slimmer than you thought, even allowing for the years – quite trim, even, in her plaid trousers and fisherman's jersey. While her style of dress is casual, this is certainly not the slut you have been led to expect from the hints that Bapty has been letting drop – where, for example, is the point of contact with that vulgar woman on the train with her handbag disgustingly crammed with used Kleenex, who called her so vividly and vehemently to Bapty's mind?

Conceivably, then, this could be the Margot of twelve years ago, perhaps before she let herself go. But it isn't. It is not Margot at all. See the oval face, still solemn although the eyes are sad no longer and she is being wryly merry about her shopping expedition. It is Ruth again, as she is now, or as you must assume she is now unless and until it is proved otherwise. Yet Bapty remains as he was then. He has done a switch, a substitute. Ruth has done Margot's shopping, now he has her commandeer Margot's sherry and greet Margot's friends – Ruth's friends, as they have become – as they banteringly raise glasses. Henry has left. Or perhaps he is still there at the Marquis of Granby bar with his pewter tankard: for it now dawns on you that Bapty has audaciously hi-jacked the entire joshing tableau and conveyed it bodily to a completely different pub. A small, snug establishment it seems – a snug, indeed, is what it is, all brass and plush, its moulded ceiling sepia with nicotine, its flock-papered walls cluttered with old prints and posters. There's another, bigger room beyond the bottle-cluttered bar, and beyond that, though you cannot see through the frosted windows with their bevelled Stars of India and engraved lettering, there is a suggestion of the sea. You have been here before, very briefly, but with the little bar in close-up where Bapty and young Oliver Pease were having their celebratory morning drink. Now you see it through a wide-angle lens. This is Winnie's Bar at The Taps, Portsea Sound's local. Both rooms are packed. Everyone seems to know Ruth and Bapty – the toast of the town, you might say. They look an ideally-matched young couple, he in his denims, she in her tartan trews and chunky sweater, and very much in love as gravely and in unison they raise their sherry schooners, their eyes exchanging promises.

This little transformation scene has got Bapty as far as Gloucester Road tube station, where he spots an empty telephone box. Telling himself that there can be only one reason why a Central London phone box would ever be found vacant, Bapty first extends the territory of the Buggerisation British Telecom sub-manager with responsibility for the Victoria pay-phones to include the Borough of Kensington, and then has unseen hands press the detonator that will blow up his East poxy Croydon bungalow with TNT.

Too late to prevent the explosion, even if he wished to, he finds that the phone does work after all. He dials, thinking still of Ruth. But the name he practises in his head, to be sure of being word-perfect, is *Margot Shepherd, please,* to which he adds, by way of spicing it up a little, *Now if I'd wanted her secretary, darling, I'd have asked for her secretary, wouldn't I?*

He gets the ringing tone, and allows it a count of two.

– Oh, there you are – so sorry to interrupt your coffee break . . .

Really: what with this and the blazing bungalow, Bapty is getting to repeat himself – and it's not yet eleven in the morning.

As if conscious of your reproving smile (although, of course, he isn't) he automatically checks his watch again, as he has done twice already in the past eleven minutes. His mind records *One more minute.* One more minute to what?

– If you can't cut your drinking down drastically, then do the sensible thing and big, dangling, hairy, horrible spherical objects – why don't you go and get yourself an estimate from a taxidermist?

Ah, yes. One more minute to opening time.

He presses home a coin, while simultaneously shutting the folding doors of the phone box with a savage kick, as if angry with them. Perhaps he is, but you are not to know why. Bapty's mind is now behind wood and glass, and sealed off for the present, like a fish in a tank.

He has got through to someone but has he got through to Margot? It is difficult to say. Peering in at him, as into an aquarium, you can see that his lips are moving non-stop, as if he is already deep in conversation with her as against just waiting for her to be brought to the telephone. But that doesn't signify – his lips spend so much of their time in motion that he could be chewing gum. He might be speaking to Margot – though she need not necessarily be aware of it – but equally he might be talking to Ruth, or Ralph Jepcott, or Henry, or Oliver Pease, or Yellowley, or Dr Windows, or Buggerisation British Telecom, or the listeners to Portsea Sound's Awkward Squad, or the Editor of *The Times*, or the Kensington and Chelsea Parking Control Office, or *The Good Food Guide*, to name but a few. He has not yet spoken to *The Good Food Guide* today. He almost certainly will, if he succeeds in getting Margot out to lunch.

His lips have stopped moving now. He waits, his mind as likely as not degenerating into that buzzing screen of scrambled signals usually defined as blank. But that, with the glass wall between you, is something you can but guess at. For the present, your only clue to what is going on in Bapty's head is Bapty's face, which fortunately is as malleable and impressionable as modelling clay. It is set in agony, like the death-mask of a torture victim, while he endures the unconscionable era of seconds that will culminate in Margot either coming or not coming to the telephone.

Animated again, released from freeze-frame, his expression now performs a windscreen-wiper swing from anxiety to expectancy, back to anxiety, back to expectancy. He touches his tie. That lopsided crack in his face as he turns up his tension-tight lips, you may be sure Bapty sees in the mirror of his mind as a fetching smile. He opens his mouth, discoloured teeth bared into a mirthless grin, and seems to be uttering a forcedly jovial greeting, like a door-to-door salesman. He nods vigorously, speaks ebulliently, listens avidly, nods again, laughs unctuously, nods, shrugs, examines the not too clean nails of his free hand while again giving voice – more tentatively now, it looks like. Doubt: relief: delight – the sequence of sensations registers as clear as traffic lights. Shooting back his cuff to consult his watch, while ruminatively sucking in his cheeks, he would seem by the interrogative raising of his eyebrows to be about to suggest a time, or possibly a venue.

No: it must be Margot who is suggesting the venue, for now, cradling the telephone receiver on his dandruff-flecked shoulder, just as he saw himself doing when illustrating his dynamism for the post-consultation benefit of Dr Windows, he tugs out a cheap ballpoint pen and his cheque book, which he uses as a notepad. Or tries to. The pen doesn't work. Bapty flings it down in disgust, leers apologetically into the telephone as he mouths a few disjointed words (and in parallel, you may be sure, mentally addresses himself to the wretched pen manufacturer), finds another pen, and jots something down as if from dictation, nodding in a confirmatory sort of way. A word or two more, several elaborate, this time affirmative nods, and he simultaneously puts away pen and cheque book while wrenching open the phone box doors and hanging up the receiver.

And thinking, as he triumphantly steps out of the phone box, *Cowbag*.

Then, kneading out the indentation of the cradled telephone receiver on the velvet of his shoulder, and catching sight of his grubby nails once more as he flicks off dandruff, Bapty thinks even more decisively, *Nailfile*.

There is a chemist only a few yards away. Stepping towards it he re-checks his watch – it has become a nervous habit with him in the last quarter of an hour or so – and logs *Twenty minutes*, pub opening time by now having been superseded by the amount of time he has in hand, presumably before making tracks for MetCable's offices.

– Good morning. I bought this pen from you only yesterday an hour ago. As you can see from this advertisement it's advertised as you can see from that display card over there, it's advertised as writing for seven miles. This in fact in fact this has written for barely seven feet. Try it yourself. No, I don't want to exchange it, thank you, I'm afraid I've lost faith in this particular product, I'd just like my money back. I see. Just fetch the manager, would you?

There is a chattering nest of Arab women at the general counter of the chemist's. Bapty, simultaneously articulating and condensing some unformed, resentful and possibly racist sentiments into the epithet *Sod,* abandons his quest for a nailfile, instructing himself not to fail to gouge the dirt out of his nails with the stiff flyleaf of his diary. Feeling in his inside pocket, where his wallet bulges, he swings his glance in the direction of the prescription counter, which is not busy at all.

– Oh, spherical objects to that!

Young Oliver Pease, hastily summoned from his duties at Portsea Sound for the sole purpose of serving as Bapty's audience during the limited run of this exclamation, leeringly guffaws as in fawning appreciation of the latest macho, devil-may-care utterance of some saloon-bar buccaneer.

Before quitting the chemist's shop doorway where he has been hovering, Bapty attempts to salve his conscience by promising himself to get Dr Windows' prescription made up at Boots in Portsea tomorrow morning. One of the innermost of his inner voices is lecturing him to the effect that he knows perfectly well he won't do any such thing when it comes to it, and that it wouldn't do him any harm to take a few tablets, but he ignores it. He cannot, however, ignore the finger-wagging Dr Windows.

– Like to reach the ripe old age of sixty, I imagine?

No point in a spirited reprise of the performance so much enjoyed by Oliver: his audience has returned to Portsea. Hand still fumbling in his inside pocket, Bapty sighs wearily; but it is his cheque book rather than his wallet containing the prescription which he now extracts from it. He locates the address he has scribbled down on it in his memory-bank A–Z London street index, and slips it away again.

– Mrs Grundy's, Buffs Court, EC4. Newish place in an alley not far from the Law Courts, much used by hacks and lawyers. Impertinent amateur waitresses incompetently serve self-consciously English food ruined by pretentious sauces, plus followed by compounded by nauseatingly-named 'Just Desserts' (sic) – Mrs Grundy's Celebrated Fig Roll etc. Over-priced wine list. Decor: fake Dickensian, no, stripped-pine chophouse.

One of Margot's haunts, it's to be presumed. If the *Must book* with which Bapty signs off his *Good Food Guide* entry happens to be true, then Margot must be booking the table, since the thought has not entered his head. What does enter his head is the possibility of her paying the bill. He seems to find something powerfully erotic in the idea.

See them nursing their Armagnac in their stripped-pine corner booth. A saucer bearing a folded bill appears on the gingham tablecloth. After a suitable pause, here pruned down to a tenth of a second, both reach for it at once. Their hands touch. Observe how Margot's beautifully-polished nails are as free of chipped varnish as Bapty's are now immaculately free of dirt. Then, slowly pulling out of this tight close-up, note the lack of lipstick daubs on her coffee cup, the ashtray empty of the bent, puffed-once cigarette stubs that always reminded him of dog-turds, and the absence of the undefined powder-puff cloud of squalor usually surrounding Margot at these reunions in the mind of Bapty. Their fingers interlock. Pan up to their faces. No, you are wrong: he has not exchanged her for Ruth this time – not exactly. He has done something even more bizarre. It is Margot all right, but with Ruth's countenance somehow superimposed on hers, so that while the facial characteristics are Margot's, the facial expression is Ruth's – the same sad, wise, haunting, elusively sensual expression as you glimpsed in that first photo-image of her to the accompaniment of Bapty's rather theatrical yearning repetition of *Ruth, Ruth*. And now he repeats *Margot, Margot* in the same overdone manner. Yet all morning on and off – as not two minutes ago – he has been thinking *Cowbag*. He is a rum customer, this Bapty.

He crosses Gloucester Road in a long diagonal, astonishing the self-employed, uninsured van driver who runs him over with the hugeness of his claim for damages. So flattered is he by Ralph Jepcott's affidavit assessing his lost earning capacity that he is positively simpering as he enters the Marquis of Granby.

Following him in, you can see at once that it is nothing like the Marquis of Granby as he has been retrospectively seeing it and as he anticipated seeing it again, although it is recognisably the same place. Where it was distinctly genuine Edwardian it is now decidedly mock-Edwardian, its fake beeswax-polish patina glistening like treacle. There are several options here. Either it has been tarted up without Bapty's knowledge in the period elapsing since his last visit; or it has been tarted up with his knowledge but without his approval, whereupon he has suppressed the change of decor either as being out-and-out unacceptable or – in that all his significant memories of the pub, including what might be termed his future recollections, pre-date the refurbishment – historically inaccurate; or it has always looked like this except in Bapty's imagination, inside which there sometimes appears to be an interior decorator trying to get out. Which?

You have the answer as Bapty's mind first voids itself in nervous preparation for a supreme effort beyond the call of duty, and then magnificently bursts forth in a kind of catherine wheel effect of mental laser beams, showering the hemisphere of his cranium with a multi-image holographic aurora borealis of grisly retribution as vast in its scale as any great battle painting, as ingenious in its cruelty as any biblical panorama of Hell. Brewers turn on spits, landlords past, present and future swing from gibbets on nooses of piano wire, hordes of french polishers, carpenters, painters and decorators and other workmen form an Appian Way of crucifixions stretching to the horizon, architects and designers are methodically flayed alive, regulars either approving of or tacitly accepting the alterations are summarily tried in batches of fifty by the League of Justice and tossed into the crocodile-crawling sewers with padlocked canvas bags over their heads. No-one escapes – save Bapty, whose Jehovah-like vision, in the few seconds it lasts, enables him to avoid thinking about anything more consequential such as the state of his health or how he ought to present the case for himself to Ralph Jepcott.

He orders a glass of sherry and looks for the corner table where he used to sit first with Margot and – before transferring his custom to Portsea – latterly, in his head, with Ruth. He feels another satisfactory glow of rage as he sees a video-game table instead. Bapty checks the time with the big reproduction wall clock. He has seventeen minutes in which to deliver his blistering three-minute talk on pub architecture for the Speaking Freely spot he has just invented for Portsea Sound.

8

Follow that cab.

This is rather awkward. Bapty, hating London cab drivers, can usually be relied upon to use public transport, even though he hates that too; but that second sherry, plus a convivial dinner with Dr Windows establishing that the old slyboots drinks as much as if not more than the next man, has left him cutting it a bit fine.

You may not share his taxi, for the driver is bound to engage him in conversation and you must not be privy to what Bapty says to anyone. You will just have to try to keep up with him.

Your assumption, probably the correct one, is that his next appointment is with Ralph Jepcott at Metropolitan Cable. Looking back on everything Bapty has thought this morning, however, it is as well to realise at this stage that nothing in Bapty's ramblings has specifically told you so. He could be going to the dentist's for all you know, having rigorously suppressed all apprehension of such a visit. That, true enough, would leave him little time for his MetCable interview before lunch: but who – the remote possibility has to be faced – is to say that it is not after all an imaginary engagement like the dinner he has just enjoyed with Dr Windows?

Should you lose him, you always know where he will be having lunch. Or you believe you do.

As to what Bapty will be thinking during his taxi ride, you have already had a broad indication from his observations during the moment when, after fuming on the pavement for a minute or two (*You mean you were only going east, my friend. I think you'll find, unless my sense of geography has gone seriously awry, that you are now only going west*), he finally sighted a vacant cab and flagged it down:

— Is it possible for you to drive me to Covent Garden in silence, or have you taken a vow of not loquacinity, loquaciousness. . . ?

— Would you mind, driver? You have now four times interrupted my concentration when I'm while I'm trying to master a very important and difficult document . . .

Something on those lines. By now he'll have the driver stamping on the brake and ordering him out of the cab. *I don't think so, my friend*, Bapty will be saying if he sticks to the script to which he was putting the finishing touches as he climbed into the cab. *However, you do have a choice. You may drive me either to my destination, without further benefit of your stupid, ignorant and intolerant views on tourists of whom I happen to be one, or to the Cab Office where I shall lodge a verbatim record of your offensive remarks, it's entirely up to—*

You have lost him at Piccadilly Circus. He could be in any one of that cluster of cabs peeling off in three directions.

At least you know from Bapty that MetCable is somewhere in Covent Garden, unless he just happened to be thinking *Covent Garden* randomly, as he might have thought *Victoria* or *World's End* or *Nottingham*. You could stop off at this hotel and look up the address in the telephone directory, but that would take time. Perhaps better to press on to Covent Garden and then ask.

You cannot blame the driver for not knowing where to go, for MetCable is very new and is not even transmitting programmes yet. There can be little doubt, though, what Bapty, in your place, would be saying in his mind. It is what he mentally observed to a cab-driver he noticed consulting a map in Old Brompton Road this morning, long before it ever occurred to him that he might have to take a taxi to MetCable's offices instead of going by tube:

— Excuse me, but do you in fact have the faintest pigging glimmer of an idea where we are going? Well yes, in fact I do in fact expect you to keep tabs on every new building on every new business in London, I thought it was part of your job.

If you can do my flaming job any better than I can, squire, you're welcome to take over, he had the cabbie saying.

– I'm quite sure I couldn't do it any worse, my friend. I most certainly wouldn't be fart-arsing around in circles like—

Wait. Tell your driver to pull up here. Open your window. Listen.

– I would have thought a five pound note, ten pound note, was a fairly common unit of currency these days. If you've genuinely just come on without any change, which by the way I would have thought was on a par with coming out without your pigging trousers, then I suggest you go into that bank over there and acquire some. Or if you're too bone-pigging-idle to get up off your bum I can by all means give you provide you furnish you with my name and address. What I certainly don't propose what I'm certainly what you're most certainly not getting is a ten pound note for a two pounds sixty fare . . .

You are in luck. There up the street is Bapty, paying off his driver who appears to be experiencing no difficulty in producing change for his proffered fiver. Bapty's lips moving servilely as he utters his thanks, while (judging by the driver's expression) handing over a too-generous tip, are in marked contrast to the lips moving viciously in his head.

This doesn't look like the place. Bapty's cab has dropped him off at the junction of a side street and an alley which between them form a jumble of small design studios and graphics workshops. Either he is not due at MetCable after all or their offices are along the street somewhere and he has been falsifying his timetable to give himself a few minutes in hand.

Yes, he has decided to walk around the block. Unless you pay your own cab off very quickly you will have to stand on the corner and wait for him to reappear. But it will be more amusing to follow him. Worth forgoing your change.

The drumbeat sound is Bapty's heart pounding. He gropes for some suitably escapist theme to think about. Schooldays. *Bapty, come out here.* Sex. *Sorry. Bit tense.* Christmas shopping in Harrods food hall, then. Cornwall. It's no good. His mind splutters, seizes up, then spirals like a stalled aircraft through cloudbanks of misted memory into an electrical storm of disjointed words and word-inventions. *Cream. Faraday. Par-parp. Hollingworth. Luggage bath. Nimp. Baglash.*

The storm calms. Now see his shoulders twitching. Bapty is singing in his head again. Vying with 'There is a tavern in the town,' a few bars of which he regaled you with while rampaging the wrong way along Old Brompton Road earlier, there has been a snatch of Percy Grainger's arrangement of 'In An English Country Garden' loitering there all morning. Unlikely that he would have heard either on Portsea Sound while shaving: they are just part of his mind's repertoire. So, called up probably by that very brief excursion into his schooldays just now, is the ballad 'Oh no, John' which he used to sing in Mrs Tate's, no, Mrs Lyle's, music lesson. Incongruously, a Percy Grainger himself for a few steps along this Covent Garden alley, he sets the words of 'Oh no, John' to the tune of 'In An English Country Garden':

– *Ho ho-ho-ho ho hohohoho no ho, no-ho John no John noh ho-ho*

No Johnny no no Johnny-nonny no no. . . .

Warbling thus as he toddles on his way, Edgar Samuel Bapty is as merry and bright as he is likely to be all day. Sad to say, not for long. It is as if his mind, recognising that he is trying to push something to the back of it yet not knowing what, malevolently begins to turn itself out like a loft, tossing ragged, festering parcels of long-concealed remembrance at his feet.

– Bapty. Come out here. Bapty, do you possess a handkerchief?

– Yes sir, you toss-bollocking four-eyed sod.

– Then for heaven's sake use it, lad!

– *Ho no-no-no no nonny nonny no ho . . .*

– Eggo. Could I have a word?

Eggo. His nickname in the old Glassborough days.

– Sure. What's on your mind?

– Well you are, to be perfectly frank. Look, don't take this the wrong way and I know it's an unconscious habit, we all do it after all but usually in private.

— What are you rambling on about?

— All I'm asking is if you wouldn't mind not picking your nose in front of the girls. They don't like it.

— What — failed the audition, have I?

— Come, on, Eggo!

— Spherical objects. I happen to have a very painful spot inside my nostril. Anyway, which sensitive soul's complaining?

— The whole bloody office staff, mate. It's all I could do to stop them getting up a petition. And I'd get that spot seen to you if I were you, because it's been giving you trouble for a very long time.

— *Ho no-no-no no Johnny-nonny no no . . .*

That poxified pratt-faced bastard Alan Twentyman. Eighteen, nineteen swining years ago that was, when Bapty was deputy assistant dogsbody at the old rat-trap studios in Glassborough, his first job in commercial radio. Every word true, every word remembered, an autobiographical strain in the fiction of his mind. Twentyman is dead now, has been for a decade or more, but that's no use to Bapty. In Bapty's mind he is immortal. Poor Bapty.

9

This looks like it – this converted fruit and vegetable ware-house. Yes. METCABLE HOUSE. Or MECTABLE SHOUE as Bapty reads it, rendered half-dyslexic by fear.

Passing through the sheet glass doors and across what seems like an acre of newly-varnished floorboards, he allows himself the brief luxury of pacing the empty fish warehouse that is now Portsea Sound Studios, while summarising his shrewd assessment of its possibilities to an executive-looking type in an expensive camelhair overcoat, who despite his grey hair looks younger than Bapty yet has the air of being very much his senior. The conversion was practically finished before Bapty's arrival at Portsea but his acknowledgement of the fact is so faint that it is clear he no longer quite appreciates how little he had to do with it.

The MetCable commissionaire's desk is such a distance away, and Bapty's report has been so concise, that having got the ear of the grey-haired man, who from the name on his office door would seem to be one L. M. Barrington, Portsea's managing director, he finds time for a further chat with him, though on a different topic.

– Come in, Edgar. I'll get straight to the point. What's this about you having talks with MetCable?

Has he been confiding in an indiscreet colleague about today's interview? (Young Oliver Pease, perhaps – in a gory little sub-plot, you have just a glimpse of Oliver's face horribly bloodied from the fearful beating-up he has just suffered.) Whether or not, Bapty does seem to be trying to placate his own anxieties as to the cat being let out of the bag. Or perhaps this is how his jittery state at the prospect of his interview chooses to manifest itself.

— Well, they've yet to appoint a contracts manager as you know, Lance, and happening to know happening to be a friend of good mates with Ralph, Rafe, Jepcott, I've been given first refusal.

— To which you've said what, if it's not a rude question?

— That I'd think about it.

— You're not happy here, then?

Enough of that for the time being. Bapty has reached the commissionaire's desk. Hang back here by this exhibition of blown-up photographs of the company's activities while he announces himself to the wooden-faced uniformed figure who so mulishly refuses to catch his eye. It is a pity that Bapty is so keyed-up, for loathing commissionaires quite as much as he loathes cab drivers he has a set piece all ready and polished for occasions like this. As it is, while the commissionaire ponderously commences his exhaustive admittance of visitors procedure, he chooses to review his own arrival procedure:

— Bapty. How are you? Bapty. How *are* you? Ralph Jepcott? Rafe Jepcott? Mr Jepcott? Edgar Bapty. Good to—

His heart as hot and freezing as a baked Alaska, he breaks off, utterly convinced that Jepcott's name isn't Jepcott at all. The name *Westmacott* drops back into his head from wherever it has been hovering for the best part of three hours, and lodges there like a fishbone in the throat. Now, realising his failure to keep the pledge made on the train this morning to check Jepcott's signature on the letter he is carrying and pokerwork it into his brain before crossing MetCable's threshold, he gets himself into such a stew that he is unable to remember not only Jepcott's name but any other name or any word in the English language. *Blark. Panch. Hafkung. Stample. Alb. Narpon. Luggage bath. Jepcott.* Furtively, he peers into the depths of his jacket as if it were soft porn concealed there in his inside pocket, and turns down a corner of Jepcott's letter to reveal his signature. Jepcott Jepcott Jepcott. Westmacott. Luggage bath. Jepcott.

– R. Jepcott? E. Bapty. Very good great pleasure to meet you, R.

See how, in tandem with his lips moving, his right arm jerks convulsively. He is practising his handshake too.

Bapty, ambling away from the desk where his name, the purpose of his visit and other essential details are being entered in a book as painstakingly and painfully as if MetCable's commissionaire were a monk transcribing the Bible, now joins you at the free-standing zig-zag of display panels, as little seeing them as he sees you. Staring sightlessly at a blown-up cross-section of a 100-channel-capability fibre optic cable and its accompanying caption, which may as well be in Hebrew for all it conveys to him, he is asking the commissionaire:

– Is it Mr Ralph or Mr Rafe Jepcott? Or don't you know?

He puts the question six or seven times in slightly different form, on one occasion with the rider *I'm talking to you, pigface*; then, having irrelevantly plucked the word *coaxial* from the mass of technical hieroglyphics in the display board caption, he is reminded by a fancied conviction that *coaxial* is a near-anagram of *Lance* that he has yet to conclude his chat with Portsea Sound's managing director.

– I wouldn't say I wasn't happy here, Lance. I just feel it's time I moved on.

– It's nothing to do with Margot, is it?

– What, about you giving her one, do you mean? Not really. Practically everyone in Portsea Sound wearing trousers has, after all. I thought it only fair to give the lads at Metropolitan Cable a chance to get their legs across.

He saunters back to where the commissionaire has unhurriedly completed his paperwork and is now unhurriedly dialling an extension number with a view to unhurriedly announcing the visitor's arrival. Bapty, rocking slightly on his heels, regards the commissionaire benevolently.

– This was your big ambition in life, was it, to sit at a desk in a peaked cap and a nice smart uniform, obstructing everyone who comes in to do business? You've done very well, sergeant.

I suppose your war service must have helped. What did you what were you, then? Trained saboteur?

You might have known that in the end Bapty couldn't resist such a sitting duck. It's probably doing him good, enjoying himself so thoroughly for the odd moment. Amoeba-like, he divides himself in two, one Bapty continuing to harangue the commissionaire, another Bapty chortlingly retailing the monologue, suitably heightened and touched-up, to some unseen audience.

– Tell me, I've always wondered something I've always wondered about. What does a failed what happens to failed commissionaires who couldn't get through the course? I mean those who just didn't have enough cotton wool between the ears?

The commissionaire brings Bapty's tauntings to a reluctant end by directing him to the lifts. You have not heard which floor he wants, but it will be quite safe to travel up with him. Since the lifts are self-operating, Bapty can speak to no-one but himself. Should he do so – aloud, that is – it will be but his own thoughts he is voicing. It will not count as hearing what he is saying.

His skull throbbing like a pressure cooker, he would very much like either to talk aloud or to burble incoherently, or even sing. It would be like releasing a jet of steam. But he holds back, hearing his voice echoing up the liftshaft through some acoustic freak, to the amusement of shirtsleeved men and office girls who roll their eyes and exchange mock-baffled glances. Bapty keeps his thoughts in his head.

– Edgar Bapty. How *are* you? We have in fact met in fact, I don't know whether you remember? That balls-aching Media-tech Conference in Birmingham, when was it, three, four years back? Bloody waste of time that was.

He's left it a bit late, hasn't he? He should have his opening lines off pat by now, yet even at this late stage he's only doodling. Did he just make that conference up or did he read about it somewhere and wish he'd been important enough to be invited to it? Bapty won't say, but it doesn't matter. His emergency pilot system has just broken in to instruct him to confine his greeting to *How do you do* and no more.

The lift boasts a mirror. Bapty pulls down his upper lip and tugs a hair out of his left nostril, the while telling himself *Cardboard. Pinpoint. Verily.* Ralph Jepcott pumps his hand:

– Edgar, good of you to stop by. I was just an hour ago only yesterday the other day talking about you with a mutual friend from your Glassborough days. Alan Twentyman?

– *Ho no-no-no no nonny nonny no, in an English country Twentyman . . .*

Waiting for Bapty while he endures his forthcoming ordeal (although he has almost certainly endured the worst of it already) should present no problems. He steps out of the lift into a great open-plan arena occupying a whole floor of the old warehouse apart from a row of executive-looking offices along the far wall. It is half reception area, half general office with a dozen or so rows of audio-typists who are presently occupied in passing round a petition against nose-picking. Screening off the lifts here is a bank of potted plants fronted by a long sofa. You may sit comfortably out of earshot and hear Bapty's thoughts as they come wafting through the fronds while he waits to be received. When the door of Ralph Jepcott's office closes upon him, of course, he will be cut off, and you will have to amuse yourself for a while.

Bapty crosses toward the imposing, company-image-conscious, boomerang-shaped reception desk, his footsteps sounding on the waxed pine floorboards, his heart thudding on the off-beat. He walks as self-consciously as if he were on stilts, keenly aware that the eyes of all the nose-picking petition signatories are upon him or would be if they were looking in his direction. The attention he is directing towards his embarrassing lower limbs also draws into his mental limelight the pelvic region. Bapty now has no alternative but to accept as correct a half-diagnosis made while going up in the lift but rejected as pragmatically unthinkable: that he desperately wants to pee – or at the very least, that he ought to have gone in the Marquis of Granby while he had the chance, and that in his

77

regret for not having done so the need will grow desperate.

Smiled into an easy chair by the glossily-attractive receptionist – her warmth generated by professional charm, he reluctantly concludes, rather than by her having fallen instantly in love with him – he picks up a trade magazine while she announces him on her intercom.

He is in Dr Windows' waiting room. Opposite him, dandled on the knee of her mother who stares across at him with unblinking hatred, cowers the diminutive victim of Bapty's anti-litter drive in Old Brompton Road, all her facial muscles twitching grotesquely as the nervous result of her court trauma. The kindly Bapty proffers a barley sugar, only to be deafened by shrieks at the rustle of its cellophane wrapping.

– Now if you take these as often as you should, Mr Bapty, there'll probably be an effect on your waterworks . . .

So Dr Windows has called him back simply to repeat his warning that the tablets he is taking will make him pee. Not that he is taking the tablets but they still make him pee. Or would, if he could find a lavatory.

– Is there a men's room on this floor at all?

– I'll just pop to the little boys' room if you'll—

– Have I time to pick my powder my nose, do you think?

Is he about to petition the receptionist? Yes. No. Yes. *Gents. Toilet. Tinkle.* The more he dithers, the more his mind floods with crude euphemisms. *Bog. Jakes. Pointing Percy at the porcelain.*

– By the way, which way is— By the way, where will I find—

Too late. She's on the telephone. The silhouetted MEN symbol stencils itself on Bapty's brain as he looks around for a door with a sign on it. There isn't one that he can see. He thinks transiently, longingly, of the vast marble urinals in the old Wine Lodge at Glassborough, where each stall was big enough to keep pigs in, then crosses his legs and tries to concentrate on his trade paper.

Cable Plugs by Networker he reads, but only with difficulty, like an infant on its first Janet and John book.

He should have gone on the train, never mind the Marquis

78

of Granby. Trying to recall why he did not, he seeks a culprit, but by now has only the shadowest memory of his annoying fellow-passengers. No matter: he'll invent one. He has already taken against one of the audio-typists – that one immediately behind and to the left of the receptionist, if you can see her from where you are, she of the thin lips, red cold-streaming nose and wire-framed spectacles. Troublemaker, Bapty has marked her down as. Branch union official. Women In Cable Media Group. Instigator of the nose-picking protest. Now he bundles her out of her chair and into the lavatory of his coach on the 8.33 from Portsea. She has been in there from Redhill to Wandsworth Common and Bapty has called the inspector.

– She is *not* doing what comes naturally as you put it, my friend. Shall I tell you what she is doing in there? She is making she is practising rehearsing going over the lines of a political speech. Now I don't know how well you know your own regulations, but occupying monopolising a toilet compartment for the purpose of sole intention of polishing up your her one's rabble-rousing remarks to the Workers' United Party of Great Britain or whatever crackpot cause it might be—

Bapty knows she will try to make him pay for this. Reaching MetCable well ahead of her he makes several decisive phone calls with the speed of light. By the time the tight-lipped tight-arsed constipated snot-snivelling four-eyed bitch storms into the office, he is ready for her. Calmly, he receives the expected news that she has called the entire clerical staff out over the most trivial of grievances – a task being assigned to someone of an inappropriate grade, something of that order: Bapty will have to work out the details later. Placard-waving pickets surround the building as Bapty enters – his second arrival in one morning. He makes one more phone call: his announcement to the Press Association that MetCable is closed down, its premises sold to become a car park. He ignores the waiting, worrying posse of union officials, headed by Miss Tightbum herself. They have had all the warnings they are getting. He strides out of the building, smashing his briefcase in the face of the demonstrator who tries to grab his sleeve. A demolition crane trundles into view, its tracks only narrowly avoiding those who would lie under it. Bapty, from a safe distance, watches. The big iron ball swings on its chain and crashes like a giant conker through the newly-repointed and steam-cleaned brick wall, exposing the area where he now sits to the gaping crowds in the street below like a room in a doll's house.

Metropolitan Cable's Ralph Jepcott says he can bring in his mixed package for around £7 a month including family entertainment, health, hobby and children's channels, plus a high street shopping channel, community channel, Prestel and availability for minority broadcasts . . .

With the effort of a child forcing down cold stew, Bapty manages a few lines more of *Cable Plugs by Networker* before beginning to regurgitate the print in gristly, undigested lumps. Premium film channel . . . viable . . . wired city . . . bedrock . . . luggage bath.

Frenetic scallop, observes Bapty conversationally to himself for want of anything else to say. *Extinguish glass. Cockatoo flooring.*

With an effort he calls his mind to order. He applies himself to the printed page again, telling himself that he really ought to read this crap. His eye, however, dances to another section headed *Appointments Round-Up*, consisting of a tightly-printed column of hazy type as it might appear to one needing glasses who is not wearing them; whereupon his mind's eye straight away locates the one legible paragraph, a modest item about himself. *Portsea's Bapty for MetCable . . .*

Or rather, it is located by Mr Grady, his old form master at Bradthorpe Grammar. Bapty wishes to impress the old sod, as he designates him, for all that he must have been dead for years now. You can tell from the duality of Bapty's momentary sensations – toe-curling pleasure twinned with stomach-churning disgust – that he makes a practice of laying little titbits of this kind at Mr Grady's feet. Apples for the teacher, the nauseated half of him calls them.

– Young Bapty goes from strength to strength, I see.

Mr Grady passes the folded journal across to Mr Carlisle, who, as in a circled inset to an old-fashioned boys' periodical illustration, can be seen jeering and railing at Bapty for not understanding algebra. What *Cable & Satellite News* is doing in the masters' common room of Bradthorpe Grammar School is not explained by Bapty's mind to Bapty, nor by Bapty to Bapty's mind.

– So I believe. I never thought he had it in him.

– No, you stupid ignorant pratt, you thought he'd spend the rest of his days in the pigging advertising department of the pigging *Bradthorpe Argus*, didn't you?

Bapty invents an uncouth sports master, loosely modelled on himself, to deliver this interjection. Conning the page for the *Portsea's Bapty for MetCable* item, which now reads *Bapty, Jepcott in MetCable Shuffle*, Mr Carlisle continues:

– Over in Glassborough still, is he?

– Good Lord, man, you're going back to the Dark Ages there! He's made tremendous the most tremendous strides since those days . . .

Bapty fades down the sound and superimposes over the common room backdrop a big tracking close-up of himself running excitedly home from school – elementary school now rather than grammar, judging by his urchin appearance.

– Mam, mam, I've got my scholarship to Metropolitan Cable!

A flickering image only here, as grained and scratched as badly-stored old black-and-white film stock, of work-worn hands folding sheets at an ironing board.

– That's nice for you, our Edgar. What do you say to that, our Donald?

But you are not to meet his elder brother, at least not yet. Even as a bile of envy, spite and simulated contempt wells up in Bapty at the prospect of Donald's first appearance today, the receptionist strides on high floorboard-clattering heels towards him.

Legs, thinks Bapty, waking to his current surroundings as from a dream. His first concern is for the state of his bladder.

Gingerly he takes a mental dipstick to it, fearful that his ability to hold off the need to pee may have so deteriorated during his absence from the present that he could be in danger of wetting himself before he is done here. The fear itself is enough to make the dormant need urgent again, but not so urgent that Bapty can bring himself to voice the request he is now framing:˙

– Would it be at all possible to make a wee detour small detour. . . ?

Heart pounding again, Bapty follows the clacking heels through ranks of juddering electric typewriters – a particular medley of sounds that lands him momentarily back in St Stephen's Hospital as the nurse leads him to his ward. Summarily firing one of the audio-typists for her slight resemblance to that same nurse, he cudgels his brain to remember what else this typing-pool set-up reminds him of – all unknowing that he has already identified the link and rigorously severed it. With an effort of will, he unwisely solders it together again. Of course! The general office at the old Glassborough studios where all the girls sat in rows and his desk was over there by the windows and Alan Twentyman's—

Bum, thinks Bapty quickly, more to erase Twentyman from his mind than because the receptionist presents an exceptionally inviting back view. *Parquet*, he thinks next, stumbling through the last line of desks which might well be unoccupied for all that he takes in of their quite attractive incumbents. *Ramble. Hep-dype. Mankin. Luggage bath.* Were Bapty ever to be hanged, such would be his last thoughts on the long walk to the gallows.

He has seen but not seen the door of the corner office suite swing open. Now, only feet away, as the receptionist stops, smiles her toothpaste smile and gestures towards it before retracing her prison wardress-sounding steps as they now seem to Bapty, he focuses. That shirt-sleeved one-man reception committee can only be Jepcott.

More youthful-looking by far than he has been imagining, even after taking two or three years off Jepcott's photograph for what can only have been reasons of pure self-mortification. The act of extending his arm to exchange hand-shakes sends a searing pain through Bapty's chest which he correctly identifies as a stab of jealousy. Then his addled brain, switching to emergency power, sends him an urgent signal: *Could be an advantage.* To which Bapty responds cunningly: *Right. Blind him with science.*

He feels smuggishly shrewd as he suffers the shirt-sleeved young man to take his arm and draw him into the private office. Yet his last thought, as Jepcott places an inch and a half of solid oak between you and the mind of Edgar Samuel Bapty, aspires no higher than *Teacake snatching.*

Unless you have something to occupy you in the neighbour-hood, there is nothing to do now but wait. He could be half an hour, even longer. You could, should you become bored, always leave and catch up with him later at Mrs Grundy's in Buffs Court where to the best of your belief he will be having lunch with Margot. But that – you cannot have failed to notice the figures 1.30 flashing in and out of his consciousness like a digital clock every time he has had occasion to consult his watch subsequent to that telephone call – is a good ninety minutes off yet. Who knows what Bapty's mind might be getting up to in that interim?

You do not have to sit so far away now that Bapty has gone into Jepcott's office. There is a demonstration cable-TV screen over the reception desk, showing the news headlines and suchlike. That should pass the time.

10

Half an hour has gone by and he's still in there. That must be a good sign from Bapty's point of view.

You will have noticed, too, a serious-looking middle management type come down from another floor and enter Jepcott's office. He has been in there ten minutes now, so it would seem that Bapty has not only cleared the first hurdle but probably the second one as well. Doubtless Jepcott's role, as chief executive, would have been to assess his overall potential as a possible addition to the MetCable team, and this newcomer, whoever he is, will be judging his capability for the specific job of contracts manager. He seemed, on that brief appearance as he bustled in with a sheaf of files under his arm, a thoroughly managerial sort of person himself, a nuts and bolts man, unlike Jepcott who looks very much the executive high-flier that Bapty, with contempt and loathing, feared he would be.

It would be interesting to know how Bapty is handling the interview. Obviously you will get his version of it sooner or later, but there is bound to be much that is garbled or distorted. A good rule of thumb, in measuring its credibility, would be to look sceptically on any words of Bapty's that strike you as urbane or clever, particularly if he has two or three stabs at phraseology or syntax. Bapty may also be depended upon (or cannot be depended upon to refrain from so doing, according to how you look at it) to suppress or re-write almost any passage that puts him in a bad or embarrassing light. Here you should look for telltale joins in the conversation – questions that seemingly do not wait for an answer, apparent non sequiturs where damaging material has been excised, abrupt references to luggage baths and so on. It will not be easy: it is a task not unlike detecting the tamperings in a doctored tape after it has been re-recorded by a skilled sound engineer. Or perhaps not quite so formidable as that: Bapty's skills in that direction are not of the highest professional standard.

Wait: Bapty's mind speaks.

– *Barking appetite reindeer pasture hopalong farthing Grimsby nightpole elevenses stickleback mash-needle blacking-top* . . .

The poor fellow is like an oscillating old wireless set. He is so wrought up he will blow a valve if he is not careful. A good thump between the shoulder blades is all he needs to get him back on normal transmission but neither Jepcott nor the other man would know that.

The three of them stand bunched outside Jepcott's doorway. There are friendly waves, but no shaking of hands, as the older but more junior of the two MetCable executives takes his leave and moves off with his bundle of files around the perimeter of the general office area towards the lifts and, presumably, his own office on another floor. Does that bode well for Bapty, or not? We shall know soon enough. Meanwhile the atmosphere seems affable enough and Bapty seems ebullient enough, but his thoughts, while he is becoming more articulate now as he simmers down a little, are still dazed and confused.

There is a maze of figures here. He appears to be doing mental arithmetic. Anything to do with a salary offer, could that be?

No, it's not money, it's time – times, rather, and time references, a whole jumble of them. Something connected with his lunch with Margot.

– Half-past one half-past one half-past one call it an hour hour and a quarter say quarter of an hour look round don't ask questions sit down say ten to one say hour and ten minutes skip coffee no drinks dentist two o'clock.

What on earth is Bapty talking to himself about? Dentist at two o'clock, did he say? But you have already established that he can't possibly have a dental appointment today – he surely couldn't have kept it dark all this long. And in any case he'll still be having lunch with Margot at that hour, or so he says.

Paradoxically, the more he calms down, the more agitated he becomes, as he continues to juggle around with this *half-past one call it an hour say* permutation, yet still without being able to take in whatever it is he's trying to arrange with himself. A timetable, it seems to be, some hasty reorganisation of his plans arising from his meeting with Jepcott and the other man. He's not proposing to cancel the Margot lunch, that much is plain, otherwise he would surely have mentioned it to himself, but he's certainly in a very anxious state about it. Is there something that now has to be fitted in before the Margot lunch? Or immediately after the Margot lunch? Surely he's not planning to get shot of her by two on the pretext of going to the dentist, when he's not due to meet her until half-past one?

There is no point in conjecturing further: it will all come out in the wash as the saying is.

Jepcott is escorting him down towards the reception area, making quite a little stroll of it as he points out features of interest around the office, or what he conceives to be of interest. You can hear Bapty responding abstractedly in his head while wrestling with whatever may be his Margot lunch problem: *Oh, yes. Salt-crust. Deepman. Matter-day. Frenchly. Luggage bath*. It is to be hoped he is vocalising this gabble in some more acceptable if not necessarily articulate form – a series of confirmatory grunts would do at a stretch.

Here they come. You should move away now, over to the lifts. It is about here, in the vicinity of the receptionist's desk, judging by the way they are dawdling while Jepcott finishes whatever he might be saying, that they will take their leave of one another – if, indeed, such is their intention. But perhaps, after all, it is not. Or have you not yet noticed that Jepcott is now wearing his jacket, where earlier he was in shirt sleeves? You may be sure he is not the kind of man who dons his jacket merely to walk a visitor down a centrally-heated office. No:

Bapty's worry concerning the Margot lunch is about to explain itself.

'Diana – I'm without Christine for the moment. Would you be an angel and see if Peel's can give us a table for three in about twenty minutes?'

There is something wrong here.

'Yes, of course, Mr Jepcott,' says the receptionist.

'Otherwise the Trat, otherwise that new fish joint. Then let Mr Horner know where to meet us.'

'Yes, Mr Jepcott.'

He turns to Bapty.

'That's if you're absolutely sure you don't have anything else on?'

Something radically wrong.

'No, truly. I do have this dentist's appointment at two as I say, but even that I could cancel. Glad of the excuse,' says Bapty.

'Never stand between a man and his dentist. But I promise we'll do our best to see you won't need Novocaine when you get there,' joshes Jepcott. And as he takes Bapty's arm: 'I'm just about to give Mr Bapty a quick guided tour, Diana. I'm sure Peel's will be fine but if not, leave a message with Stan in the lobby.'

'All right, Mr Jepcott.'

He steers Bapty in the direction of the lifts. *Do not follow.* Let them get back out of earshot.

As Bapty is ushered away, you are able – though going strictly by the rules you are no longer entitled – to connect with his thoughts again:

– There isn't such a thing as a bog handy before we start, is there?

Never mind Bapty's bladder, though. There is something wrong and Bapty knows there is something wrong. He has that feeling, an inward shiver, usually described as somebody walking on one's grave. He looks apprehensively around as if expecting a ghost at his heels.

You have trespassed on Bapty's conversation. Everything

that has just been said was spoken, as it were, within quotation marks – that is to say, out loud. You were not supposed to be within listening range.

Perhaps you were lulled by your conviction that Jepcott and Bapty were about to say their good-byes. It could have done no harm, you may have thought, to eavesdrop on a handshake. Perhaps you then did not realise quickly enough that Bapty was about to speak. Perhaps, even, you did not comprehend until it was too late that it was in fact Bapty's voice you were hearing. It is, to be sure, vastly unlike the one you have been hearing previously and may hope to hear again if this lapse is not repeated – which is to say, since his mind is not equipped with a larynx and vocal chords, the one which he and you have been imagining. Bapty's voice is much lighter than the voice that vibrates in his skull – incongruously so, like a small head on a large body.

It is as well that nothing of consequence was said during this deviation from the agreed procedure. Little, if the truth be known – beyond the actual name of the restaurant – that hasn't already been leaked by Bapty's mind, were you adept enough at deciphering.

Half-past one call it an hour hour and a quarter. Half-past one, as you know, is the time at which he has arranged to meet Margot. But he must allow an hour to an hour and a quarter for lunch with Jepcott and the other man, Horner as his name turns out to be. *Say quarter of an hour look round don't ask questions.* Allow fifteen minutes for Jepcott's guided tour of the building, being careful not to prolong the proceedings by requests for supplementary information. *Sit down say ten to one say hour and ten minutes skip coffee no drinks dentist two o'clock.* Reach the restaurant, on his reckoning, by 12.50, or one hour and ten minutes before Bapty is supposed to be due for that bogus dental appointment you heard him lay claim to. By declining aperitifs and coffee he should therefore, he seems to be hoping, be able to join Margot at two o'clock. Though to what purpose, since he will already have lunched and she hardly sounds the kind of woman to drum her fingers for half an hour, he does not say. Perhaps he is proposing to ring her restaurant from his restaurant and make his apologies, in the hope of being invited to join her for the coffee he will be forgoing, on her behalf, with Jepcott and Horner. He does not, or did not when you last had access to his thoughts, seem altogether clear on that point.

What is clear, however, or should be, is that by application you could have learned as much and more from Bapty's mental reckonings as from the scrap of conversation you no doubt unwittingly, perhaps even unwillingly, overheard. The incident is closed now: no harm, after all, has been done. But it must not happen again. You may not follow Bapty as Jepcott conducts him around the MetCable studio complex, for they will be engaged in continuous talk and voices carry in these lofty, foot-echoing chambers. Neither must you risk waiting for them down in the lobby – Jepcott is plainly the type who attracts telephone messages wherever he goes, and there is bound to be so much conversational activity around the commissionaire's desk as they prepare to set off for lunch that you could not help but eavesdrop again.

The best thing you can do is to see if you can get a table at Peel's, wherever that may be, and await their arrival there. Or the Trat. Or that new fish joint.

II

It will be surprising if he doesn't have something to say to *The Good Food Guide* about Peel's in due course. Sloane Rangers playing at waitresses, a nouvelle cuisine menu, sea-salt on the tables – just the kind of place Bapty detests, though to be fair he detests most restaurants. And furthermore, with its stripped pine booths and chequered tablecloths, almost the double of how he's been imagining Mrs Grundy's, where he's supposed to be having lunch with Margot not thirty minutes hence, the guided tour of MetCable evidently having taken longer than he bargained for. It can't be very good for Bapty's digestion, all this.

What does he finally mean to do about Margot? He can't have done anything thus far, for having sworn he had nothing else on this lunchtime, it would have been a very cryptic call indeed for him to get away with ringing her from MetCable without Jepcott rumbling his game. He must be hoping there's a payphone here at Peel's. But he's cutting it fine, now. Whatever he's decided must involve some change in their arrangements, and at such short notice Margot isn't going to be best pleased.

Still, that's Bapty's problem. Yours is to get yourself placed as far as possible from Jepcott's table. His name jotted in the scribbling-diary on the cash desk confirms that MetCable's receptionist has succeeded in getting one but it doesn't say which. The restaurant is less than half-full so far and the MetCable party could be seated just about anywhere.

See if that table over there by the men's room is available – Jepcott clearly being one of their regulars, they surely won't put him at this end of the room between the lavatories and the kitchens. It's not the best of positions but that matters little since nobody is going to serve you (for as far as the staff are concerned – did they but know – you can exist only as a guest of the mind of the guest of Ralph Jepcott, when he deigns to arrive). At least you will be out of the way, and you are well placed to get a good look at Bapty as he hurries into the gents. He has been dying to go for coming up to an hour now, unless in desperation he finally got round to releasing a verbal transcript of one of the hundred versions of the urgent supplication in his head.

They are arriving. Horner, rubbing his palms together in a hand-washing pantomime as is the way of management men when entering a restaurant; Bapty copying him as if politely emulating the customs of a Japanese client; Jepcott looking young enough to be the son of either of them, yet imperceptibly carrying the air of a puppeteer manipulating two marionettes. The chief executive of Metropolitan Cable TV hangs back, ever so slightly aloof, while his inferior organises the table.

All this must be good news for Bapty. Everything is going so astonishingly well that the boardroom cigar of his Pullman-Yellowley whimsy could almost become a reality before the day is over. If he has not yet been offered the job in so many words, they are scarcely about to give him lunch in order to break the news that he has not got it. He should, by rights, be relaxedly looking forward to the celebratory toasts and roguish little speeches welcoming him to the madhouse. Yet what is Bapty thinking, in his garbled, hysterical way, as the young woman he has absently, mildly categorised as a pigging Hooray Henrietta bloody Roedean hockey captain titless wonder conducts them to their table?

– Skip first course Perrier water bit of fish tooth bothering day of all days phone sorry break this up got to get to that bloody dentist fast cab sorry late love skip first course glass of wine bit of steak . . .

Can Bapty be serious? Is he really intending to gollop down two lunches, one at Peel's and the other at Mrs Grundy's, as the only solution to his dilemma? Dr Windows shall hear of this.

He means it, though. Already he is cobbling the anecdote together, for the edification of a circle of admirers in Winnie's Bar:

– But you see what else could I do? I daren't turn them down – I mean talk about biting the hand that's offering to feed you, it would have been like saying stick the job up your corporate arses. And then again, there was absolutely no way on God's earth of getting hold of Margot . . .

Even as he fleshes out the story with implausible detail, Bapty, in the service quarters of his mind, is busily, pragmatically working out in what way he is likely to get hold of Margot. Buffs Court being only three or four minutes' walk from her newspaper office, she shouldn't have set off for Mrs Grundy's yet: but that's assuming the cowbag is in the office in the first place and not flat on her back with her latest assignment. Or she could be having a quick drink at the Savoy American Bar with her next lover, arranging to meet him after she has got rid of Bapty. All right: try office first, if out leave message with restaurant, asking her to ring this number. Which number? Apprehensively he looks around to establish a payphone, praying that it is not within earshot of his hosts' table.

It is not. More to the point, neither are you. Watch the three men go through the palaver of sitting, Horner deferentially holding Bapty's chair and Bapty hovering indecisively, uncertain whether to seat himself before Jepcott, who in turn waits with superior deference for his guest to sit down. Bapty, now suddenly fearful of becoming an innocent victim in a ghastly intestinal civil war in which the compelling need to break wind overpowers the compelling need to pee, at last hastily takes his seat.

With much chair-scraping and shaking out of napkins they get themselves settled down, Bapty facing the two MetCable men like a candidate at an examination, which is what he nervously feels like, but only in the very back of his mind.

What Bapty is really thinking, as he takes in a bowl of radishes on the table – or rather what his mind is thinking for him while he prepares to resume wrestling with the problem of his lunch-date with Margot – is *What big radishes*.

The Roedean hockey captain remains at the table, distributing menus and evidently taking drink orders, for you hear Bapty sternly instruct himself:

– Leave most of it.

You may depend upon it that despite hastily-framed good resolutions about skipping aperitifs and sticking to Perrier water, he has ordered a dry sherry, his third today so far. Dr Windows won't like it. Indeed, Dr Windows doesn't. He disapproves strongly of Bapty's whole course of action, so strongly that words fail him as he throws out his hands to semaphore despair.

– Spherical objects the texture of coconuts.

Jepcott, not a man to keep silent for long, commences to talk – a joke or story judging by his audience's anticipatory hovering smiles. When it comes to the sycophantic laughter for the punchline, however, Bapty will have to take his cue from Horner, for there is so much interference in his head that Jepcott's voice crackles and fades as on a ship's wireless during an electrical storm. Nodding to indicate that he is absorbing and relishing the narrative, Bapty is so desperate for it to end – either so that he can go and pee or go and telephone or possibly both – that the only message he is capable of receiving through his mind-static is that in being irresistibly reminded by Horner's name of the old nursery rhyme . . .

– *Little Jack Horner*
Sat in his corner
Eating his curds and whey;
There came a big spider . . .

. . . he has somewhere gone off the rails. Now, for one long moment, the task of locating the exact point at which the misquotation begins, and thereby hopefully ending all his accumulated anxieties, takes priority with Bapty over the MetCable job, Margot, Ruth, his high blood pressure, his need for a pee, and anything else he could think of were he capable of thinking it while the problem remains outstanding.

– *Eating his Christmas pie;*
There came a big spider—

Only fractionally behind Horner's explosive guffaw, Bapty throws back his head in a salvo of dutiful snorts as Jepcott slaps the table to punctuate the denouement of his story. The elusive nursery rhyme character connected with the big spider, whose name he was a moment ago striving to remember as frantically as if it were a magic password, is now consigned to the incinerator of oblivion along with Little Jack Horner and all his works. What is of paramount importance to Bapty now is to get to his feet before either of his companions has the chance to launch into a further anecdote.

He has forgotten about the lavatory for the moment. It is the telephone he wants most. He reminds himself foxily to be able to come up with some good reason for making a call – it won't do for Jepcott and Horner to suspect that he's got himself into the mess of having to cancel a lunch engagement on the sly.

– Is there a blower telephone payphone here at all? I've yet to ring in to my office today and of course the old bleeper doesn't work at this range.

Bapty is inordinately pleased with this line. It will make him sound indispensable. He must think it's so good it can't be improved on, for no alternative presents itself in the lengthy fraction of a second before he speaks. A rueful wag of the head from Jepcott, as one workaholic to another, is proof that the ruse has gone down well. Horner half-turns in his seat and points, Kitchener-like, seemingly at you. The payphone must be in the cloaks lobby dividing the two sets of lavatories beyond your table.

Rising as he nods his thanks, Bapty observes in passing, *Ear-pluck*, an oblique, disparaging reference to the hairs he has just noticed growing out of Horner's left ear. Unaware of having incurred his company's guest's disgust, Horner nods vigorously back, thanking Bapty for his thanks. It is not yet plain what precise role this Horner plays in the affairs of

Metropolitan Cable. It will be revealed soon enough. You will get it out of Bapty.

There is, you ought to observe while Bapty is still crossing the room, plotting sickening revenge on Buggerisation British Telecom's arson-prone sub-manager should the phone prove to be out of order, only a curtain across the entrance to the cloakroom where he will be making his telephone call. That means that although Jepcott and Horner are comfortably out of earshot, you will probably be uncomfortably within it. Something must be done here.

Bapty is passing you now, thinking:

– Will she be back before lunch at all? Look, I wonder if you could possibly get hold of her and give her—

You cannot wander about the restaurant, getting in the way of the waitresses like the Invisible Man. You had better hide in the lavatories until he has finished.

12

Now here, should you happen to be of his sex (or even should you not be, if it wouldn't embarrass you, for he cannot see you) comes Bapty now, having decided to have that pee after all.

This could be quite useful. There should be instant and informative feedback from his telephone call to Margot without the distortion you would get out in the restaurant where the MetCable business will be clamouring for equal time in Bapty's brain. It will be nice to be able to plan ahead a little.

But first, as you would expect, he registers relief at being able to relieve himself. Alas for Bapty: his memory cells, as malignant as any cancer cells, allow him just this one luxuriating second before yanking him back to re-live, in all its hideous detail, the last time he nearly didn't make it – when, in fact, by any conventional yardstick he conspicuously and disastrously failed to make it.

It is Oliver Pease's Christmas party at his flat in Winter Gardens Crescent, and some lame-brained green Chartreuse swilling upchucking cock-teasing secretary has barricaded herself in the bathroom. Bapty, with most of a box of warm Californian white wine inside him, is reduced to peeing in a vase in the broom-cupboard. It sounds like a cistern filling and seems to be taking as long, until Bapty is forced to crash his urethral muscles into reverse for fear of the thing overflowing. The emergency stop is not so complete that he doesn't feel a trickle down his leg as he zips up.

Sweating on this horrific, high-fidelity remembrance, Bapty tries what is surely a familiar trick to his memory – reprocessing the experience to give it a bohemian, raffish air, a throwback to provincial bed-sitter romps from the old Glassborough days. Memory will have none of it. Even as he slips into the old pub-crawling corduroy jacket that seems more appropriate for the part than the salmon-pink linen job he was wearing that night, memory interpolates beneath it the steaming vase which it makes him carry leaking and slopping like a smuggled bedpan into the now vacated bathroom. And if Bapty does not care to follow the episode through to its grisly end, where he returns to the party stinking (so he believes) of urine and feeling compelled to keep asking loudly which clumsy sod has spilled wine down his jacket, then, so memory hints heavily, there are other reminiscences in the same series, but even more horrendous, that it could bring out for his delectation.

— *As I was going to Strawberry Fair,*
Ho John no John hoho no-no-no John,
I met a man who was not there
With a Ho! . . .

Casting out his memory like the devil it is, Bapty stares into the wash-basin mirror, baring his teeth and grimacing and carrying out a nostril-hair spotcheck. Still shaken by what happened at Oliver Pease's Christmas party, he has Oliver and all potential tittle-tattles present die in a pneumonia epidemic, then completes the exorcism process by placing his face so close to the mirror that his nose appears to meet its reflection, and chanting to himself aloud in a high-pitched chuckling monotone like an amused monk at mass:

'*Hingle fafty mar glumph viggle noy sprat shangilibble,* *namino donkile tung—*'

He stops, petrified, so abruptly that the next nonsense-syllables in the sequence, *fash maldirundle*, tumble into his now-mute consciousness like turnips over the tailboard of a suddenly-braking farm lorry.

Something is wrong again. Is he aware of your presence? He is aware of *a* presence, that's for sure. He tingles, his back hairs bristle, not with fear but with an alert awareness, like a night animal hearing a twig crack. Slowly – although he can perfectly well see over his shoulder through the mirror – he turns, his whole body rotating inch by inch as on a hand-cranked turntable, arms stiffly by his side, until he faces you.

He does not see you, but he senses you – or he senses something, it is difficult to say for certain, since Bapty's mind is as petrified now as his person was a moment ago.

Perhaps your being in here is a mistake. He has given tongue, and you have heard him. True enough, what Bapty might say aloud to himself in lavatories, lifts and such places is supposed to be classed as pure, unadulterated thinking under the rules, and so it should not count as being overheard. But rules are open to interpretation. It comes to this. Had Bapty's nervoustic ramblings just now been confined to his head instead of being granted the liberty of his voice-box, you would probably have thought no more about them than about his routine *luggage bath* doodles which serve to lower his mental temperature when the steam is metaphorically coming out of his ears. Does his translating them into speech disturb you in any way? If so, that may be why you are disturbing him.

It is your own mind that has to be considered for a moment. If Bapty now said aloud, in matter of fact tones, into the mirror, 'I am so ashamed by what I had to go through at Oliver Pease's party last Christmas that if I thought anyone knew about it I would wish them dead to prevent them telling' – or more coldbloodedly, 'I would like to get hold of the chap who redesigned the Marquis of Granby and put his eyes out' – would that affect any policy decision of yours regarding Bapty, any opinion of his worth or unworth you may have formed so far? Would you modify or qualify whatever your reaction was when he made those or similar observations to himself, in the privacy of his own head? That is really the question. If Edgar Samuel Bapty does sense you, or if he senses that he may have been in some way overheard or understood by some person or some presence, then he will be as embarrassed and mortified as if you had been witness – say – to the cringing scene with Margot where, perhaps pleading and begging from what you are able to gather, he put the case for her transportation to Portsea – a scene so painful and humiliating to him that, after its ruthless retailoring into matinée comedy, scarcely a line of the damning original remains.

Now it is because he fears your judgment that he feels so – if feel so he does. If indeed he does so do, then he will fear your judgment mortally. You see he does not know who you are or what you are, and so he cannot alter, arrange, doctor, improve, process to his own rigid specifications your character assessment of him as he would process, for example, the character assessment of Dr Windows or Ralph Jepcott or any passing stranger, should he suppose it to be damaging, lukewarm or otherwise unacceptable. They are easy game but you are not. You lack the essential tangibility which is his raw material, this being the clay on his madly-spinning potter's wheel. Taking you on would be like trying to tamper with the judgment of God himself.

What it all comes down to of course, to get it into proportion as Bapty stands stock-still here in the lavatory like a mesmerised man with an anaesthetised brain, is that he is painfully conscious – or would be, if he allowed himself to be conscious of anything – of having just made a raging fool of himself with that *hingle fafty mar glumph* nonsense. It couldn't be worse had he been found Morris-dancing in private – that's what he's in such a sweat about. If only you can make him believe that you – or whoever or whatever he imagines you may be or could be – think no worse of him for it, or better, that you have no knowledge of it, or better still, that you are not even here, then no damage may perhaps have been done.

All clear. Bapty's mind is functioning again. He dismisses you – rather impertinently, you may consider – as indigestion, thereby despatching you to the rubbish-tip of the inexplicable where Bapty's moments of *déjà vu*, possible extra-sensory perceptions and suchlike phenomena are habitually dumped. He turns back to the mirror, earnestly picking his nose while thinking what he ought to think next.

That telephone call, Bapty. What happened?

– Tell you the truth, chaps, I should never have left Glassborough at all but for that shit Alan Twentyman getting up my nostrils – almost literally, by the way. Yes, he had this mucus complex as I believe it's called – totally obsessed with nose-picking. Pity, I was very happy there. I suppose I'd be general manager by now.

Come along, Bapty, this won't do. It can't be anywhere remotely near the truth. You only have to check the potted c.v. he is still carrying in his head in case he has to refer to it again during lunch. Joined admin side of local BBC, Glassborough, from *Bradthorpe Argus* advertising department at age twenty-four. Went across to Glassborough Radio when commercial station opened twenty years ago. Nose-picking trouble, as has been established, was eighteen or nineteen years ago. Did not join Thames Radio until he was thirty-seven, or five years later. Switched to Portsea Sound when Margot trouble came to a head ten years after that, or nearly three years ago. Nothing to do with Twentyman at all. He has not even been accused of sleeping with Margot. Not that he could ever have even met her, but Bapty wouldn't let a detail like that stand in his way.

What he means is that he was very happy up in Glass-borough until Twentyman spoiled it all for him, but he didn't have the initiative to move until Juney walked out on him. There she is doing it – and there now, seen in the mirror of his mind which can sometimes reflect as clearly as the wash-basin mirror into which he is now grimacing, is Bapty himself packing, while pretending to the mildewed ceiling that he's walking out on her. Not in so many words but in so many pangs of self-denigration he admits to himself that it was two failed marriages drove him out of Glassborough. Why they failed he isn't saying, but it must be a worse embarrassment than nose-picking, if he has to half-sublimate his blushes by putting all the blame on Twentyman.

But what, apart from passing a second or two while he rolls the scourings of his right nostril into a small pellet and flicks it away, is the purpose of these Glassborough ramblings in the first place?

– I wasn't stretched up there, that's the top and bottom of it.

All right, the going could be tough sometimes but I could do it on my head in my sleep one hand tied behind my—

What is Bapty going on about now? Why does he seem at long last to be conducting a serious rehearsal of his party piece for Jepcott? Surely they must have gone far beyond that stage or they wouldn't be here.

– I think one thing feather in the cap I can claim about Radio Thames is that when I arrived there were one and a half people doing one job each job, but by the time I left each one person every person was doing what used to be had previously been a job and a half. . . .

He's revising. Improving. Correcting. The cassette of the actual interview he somehow stumbled through will in due course be erased, and this one substituted. Though why he should put himself to the trouble, since he seems to have got away with it, is difficult to say. Perhaps he's just concerned with making good a spot of shoddy workmanship.

He washes his hands, examining his fingernails and digging them into the soap for want of the nailfile he failed to buy, and having neglected to follow his directive to scrape them out with the corner of his diary flyleaf. Absently, although his hands are already soapy, he tips the soap dispenser into his palm.

But absent-minded though the gesture may have seemed, Bapty's mind misses nothing. Bapty thinks:

– Little things. For example, noticing that there was both soap and liquid, ordinary soap and liquid soap in the lavatories. By cutting out liquid soap ordinary soap one of those soap contracts I was able to save that company three hundred four hundred two hundred and fifty pounds a year.

Wiping his hands on the roller towel, and his eye catching the hot-air hand-drier next to it, he's about to carry his cost-economy campaign further, but something more urgent is now signalling for attention. As you follow him out into the restaurant Bapty is thinking:

– No, when I said there were domestic reasons for going to Portsea accepting the Portsea post, don't get me wrong, that was just one factor new company ground floor challenging position bags of responsibility fool not to have taken it . . .

So that's where he thinks the interview could have gone better, is it? Well, he has plenty of time to put that right, even within the limits of the tight schedule he has drawn up for himself. Obviously, putting together this substitute material must take precedence over anything he might wish to think touching on what transpired on the telephone just now. It cannot have been anything of any consequence, such as Margot cancelling the lunch, otherwise it would have registered. Most probably he hasn't been able to reach her yet.

Bapty rejoins his companions, rubbing his hands in kow-towing deference in a re-run of the ceremony copied from Horner. During his two minutes' absence the aperitifs have appeared and the Roedean hockey captain stands in attendance while Horner consults his menu. Jepcott, Bapty concludes, has already ordered, thereby giving him the opportunity of asking toadingly:

– What's Ralph ordered what have you ordered Ralph what does Ralph what would you recommend Ralph what's Mr Jepcott ordered I'll have whatever Mr Jepcott's what would you advise Ralph?

Evidently he has got the Ralph-Rafe question sorted out to his satisfaction, if not the one he is poised to ask. Abandoning these sycophantic variations, Bapty picks up his menu and for the first time has leisure enough fully to appreciate the hateful-ness of the establishment to which he has been brought and all concerned with it.

– Is it not in fact possible to have what I would like to eat rather than what your chef would like to cook, bearing in mind that I am the customer and that it is not my function to indulge his pigging hobbies, especially at the prices quoted here?

He's got it off pat, that one. Such an old chestnut of Bapty's is it that, barely bothering to hear himself think it as he studies the menu, he has room in his head for a parallel and corrobora-tive strain of abuse on the particular pretentious and poncified fare on offer.

Unable to decide, he allows Horner to order first, then – prompted by a passing twinge in the chest: tensed-up muscles, he expects, it comes and goes – further allows him to die of a heart attack from over-eating. *Cable Plugs by Networker* announces the news: *MetCable's Edgar Bapty, after only a year two years three years as contracts manager, to succeed the late Peter Horner as general manager.* So now we know Horner's place in the scheme of things. Thank you, Bapty. He had better order the first of his day's lunches now (not counting, of course, the several he has already consumed in his imagination).

It is not clear what Bapty has decided on having, since his instructions to the Roedean hockey captain are obscured by his concern with manufacturing an excuse about being on a diet (a voluntary, non-medical diet, for Jepcott's benefit), should she chide him for ordering so little.

– I won't, Ralph, thanks, I'll just stay with my sherry, but don't let me stop you two.

This is as Jepcott takes possession of the wine list. Now, with Jepcott asking or about to ask the question to which he has just furnished the answer, Bapty revises his position:

– Oh, red, white, whatever. I'll go with the meeting. Shrivelled spherical objects.

Dr Windows, you will notice, is included in the projected discussion. Jepcott can be seen ordering the wine. Bapty can be heard doing the same, but more eruditely. The Roedean hockey captain moves away, in happy ignorance of one of her clientele's shouted taunts about her thick legs. The three men raise their glasses, Jepcott and Horner toasting Bapty in Campari and Scotch respectively. There is an air of congratulatory euphoria here. He thinks:

– What does rather chuff me is that there must have been a short list of at least twelve, so by no stretch of the imagination could they be accused of be said to be settling for what they could get . . .

But to which company this tribute is addressed, if any in particular, you are not to know, for Bapty has floated off on clouds of self-esteem to the flat in Viceroy Court with all his old Colchester Place Mansions furniture intact, and silver, cut glass and London Cries place mats all prettily laid out on the long mahogany dining table – now upgraded to Queen Anne again – for the dinner party he is throwing for the Ralph Jepcotts and Peter Horners.

– Ruth you haven't met . . .

Elegant in a blue satin evening gown – either Bapty has a good eye for dress design, or it has previously been modelled for him, perhaps by Margot – Ruth steps forward to greet her guests, even as, in tandem, the Roedean hockey captain steps back to the table and speaks to Bapty. Like a picture-card of an apple or a zebra held up in front of a child learning the alphabet, a simplified symbol of a telephone slides over the bonhomous scene.

Let the cowbag wait, thinks Bapty, nodding an acknowledgement and saying something to his hosts, or guests as they half-remain in his head.

That explains why he wasn't thinking about Margot when he entered the men's room. There was nothing to think: he rang her but she wasn't there, or was on another line, and so he asked if she would ring him back. He put her on hold, so to speak.

He is not thinking very much about her even now. Half-rising, still talking, he has a vision not of Margot but of young Oliver Pease on the other end of the line. He is obviously spinning them some yarn about how he cannot leave the office for a minute.

Striding down the restaurant, gleaming with self-importance, Bapty rosily conjectures what Jepcott and Horner might be saying about him in his absence:

– Seems quite a live wire, Peter.

Interesting that he still gives Jepcott the livewire mid-Atlantic accent with which he endowed him before he ever heard him speak, even though you know from that unfortunate episode back at MetCable that it sounds nothing like him. Horner, in contrast, and probably just as inaccurately, he

makes a slow-talking dullard, fashioned somewhat after
Henry:

– Yerss, yerss, I reckon we could go further and fare worse as
the saying goes. How long would we do we have to wait for
him?

– Fortunately for us, his contract has run out and he's wisely
refused to renew it.

– Yes, well I couldn't really continue to tie myself down with
a tinpot little small, rather, small station like Portsea which
however first rate I could only regard as a springboard . . .

(Bapty himself speaking: miraculously, he has joined in the
conversation in his own absence.)

– In fact, gentlemen, to be perfectly blunt and without being
disloyal, had it not been for my domestic circumstances at the
time, I probably wouldn't have entertained them in the first—

As Bapty passes you, so a shadow passes across his mind, at
once filling him with unfocussed, momentary dread, yet shield-
ing him from the source of it, which is that frisson of trepidation he felt at your presence – or whatever he believed your
presence to have been – back there in the lavatory where you
took refuge while he made his phone call.

There is no need to move on this occasion. He is not heading
for the payphone: it's to be assumed he asked for Margot to
ring him back at the restaurant's own number on the bookmatch he has pocketed in anticipation of a celebratory cigar.
He is ushered through a door marked Private.

Jepcott and Horner, it may be judged from Horner's occasional apprehensive glances over his shoulder to check against
Bapty's return, certainly are talking about him just as he
anticipated, though perhaps not in the complimentary terms
he allowed himself to imagine. Jepcott seems to be canvassing
his general manager's opinion. Horner, with an indecisive wag
of the head and a seesawing motion of the hand, does not seem
entirely persuaded in Bapty's favour. Jepcott, probably influenced by the other man's doubts, now looks doubtful
himself, shrugging up his shoulders and rocking to left and
right, his hands in the posture of a juggler's as he holds some

question in the balance. Horner speaks. Jepcott looks round almost furtively, then speaks back, leaning across to Horner so as not to be overheard. Both MetCable executives laugh, coarsely. Has a joke been made at Bapty's expense? Certainly there is a suggestion here that the outcome of his interview may not be the foregone conclusion he believes.

Bapty returns, his head so alive with arrangements that he experiences barely a pang of foreboding as he brushes past you. *Leave here quarter to two ten to two fast cab five to two must get to bank ten to two say dentist's in Harley Street Wimpole Street . . .*

He rubs his jaw ostentatiously as he goes back to his table. *Tooth playing me up*, he means to say, but doesn't, hoping the message has been adequately conveyed. He resumes his seat, looking pleased. Bapty's mind is split screen again. On one side, full of the panic stations call he is pretending to have just taken from Portsea, he is instructing Oliver to get that drunken sot Valentine off the premises and take the phone-in programme himself; in the other he is descending a flight of steps into Mrs Grundy's restaurant, which in view of Peel's close resemblance to it he has now had completely redesigned to resemble the Captain's Table in Portşea. He throws open his arms in an elaborate gesture of apology as he perceives Margot sitting at the best table in the house with an ashtray of cigarette butts and what is probably her third gin and tonic. The image of Oliver is erased, presumably as Bapty concludes his account of what he wishes his companions to believe his telephone conversation was in connection with. Margot now takes up the whole screen.

They are not in the restaurant any more. They are in someone's flat – hers, most likely, since she seems to know where the drink is kept. She presses a glass of Armagnac into his hands, her face very close, her smile distorted as if seen through the fish-eye lens of the brandy glass. Margot now appears to be sporting provocative long black velvet gloves, which she most certainly wasn't wearing at the lunch he is about to go to when he has had the lunch he is at. She shimmers off into what is presumably her bedroom, and Bapty comes comparatively back into MetCable's orbit.

Yes, he is replying in his head, though in answer to what he does not know. *Yes. Yes. Quite.* Jepcott has said something to him, he has no idea what. Now Horner speaks too. Bapty adopts a listening attitude but he will not, cannot, properly listen. He thinks:

– Champagne is called for, wouldn't you say?

Is this to Margot? It is certainly not to his future colleagues, as he is confident they are. His co-celebrator is identified as an alarm bell rings in Bapty's head:

– RING RUTH.

The shock brings him to the realisation that Jepcott has asked him a direct question and is waiting for an answer, though he has only the vaguest idea of what has been said. Bapty's mind is leading him on to very thin ice here: he is auditioning for a senior appointment and he doesn't even take in what his interrogators are asking him. It is to be hoped he kept his thoughts better in check during his formal interview.

It was something to do with the theatre. Does he go to it much, or has he seen some particular show? Bapty, under cover of clearing his mouth of the bread roll he has been scoffing in the self-denying absence of a first course, throws together the beginnings of an answer:

– I'm not a big theatre man, frankly. For one thing I don't have the time the way I'm professionally situated, and for another, don't we all have a theatre in our own living rooms these days, particularly with the onset of cable. . . ?

It's the wrong, philistine, answer and he knows it, as it now seeps into his intelligence that his companions have been talking about the National Theatre, which Jepcott and his general manager both seem rather to approve of. Nevertheless, he lets his reply through almost unedited, hardly bothering even to monitor it as, with his voice safely on auto, he thinks to himself in the persona of his brother Donald, now seen as a thinner, older replica of himself:

– Bloody good, our kid. So when I get sick of teaching or

teaching gets sick of me whichever be the sooner, I can count on a bit of nepotism should I come down to London job-hunting . . .

His mother joins in the clamour of congratulations, as does a woman from the far distant past he can't quite place – a relative or neighbour. He is none too sure how he has rounded off his views on the theatre, such as they are, but he can see that they have not made much of an impression on Jepcott and Horner, who begin to talk among themselves about some production they have seen and admired. Concerned at being frozen out, Bapty does his best to concentrate, gulping down words and phrases like pills – *choreography – actor who was in – director – night we were there – understudy* – but it all means nothing to him, and soon he is weaned away, soothing himself with a kind of lullaby of nonsense:

– Consequential Remington. Half below moccasin. Flea-bone armadillo. Oh, lute harp positive. Luggage bath.

The main courses have arrived, delighting yet dismaying Bapty by the size of the portions. If he does full justice to his steak in a mustard sauce, he will not be able to look at a lunch with Margot, let alone eat it. If he leaves half of it, he will offend his host, as well as the ratbagging spoon-faced tree-trunk-legged Roedean hockey captain, who is bound to be tiresome. Nothing is thought about his earlier resolution to toy with a little fish.

– Jesus, this tooth. Excuse me, sudden stab of pain like a red hot—

No. Won't do. They'll put him down as a whiner. He chomps, waving a fork to indicate his appreciation, and allowing Horner to pour him a second glass of wine despite his determination to drink only one.

There is a lull. Bapty feels, knows, that it is up to him to inject a lively note into the conversation but, in the grip of a sudden inertia as all-embracing as a foam-rubber octopus, he can think of absolutely no contribution to make beyond the words *Burberry raincoat* which he wisely does not introduce. A superior, sabotaging part of his brain is telling him that his real priority should be to find a way of decently leaving a good part of his steak.

– No, I'm sorry, gentleman – excellent though that was, I'm afraid I must confess myself defeated . . .

– That was one of the finest steaks I've ever tasted. This sauce is delicious. However. . . .

Bapty eats up his steak, mopping up after himself with a speared morsel of bread while holding a conversazione with his late mother, Dr Windows, Mr Grady of Bradthorpe Grammar and others, and at the same time writing to *The Good Food Guide* about undercooked vegetables. He pays perfunctory, desultory attention to Jepcott and Horner. It does occur to him that they, for their part, seem now to be paying only minimum attention to him also, but he is too cocooned in self-congratulatory lethargy to care. His leaving party at The Taps, overflowing from Winnie's Bar into the adjoining bar and up the stairs, is in full swing. He hardly notices the two newcomers to Peel's who have paused at Jepcott's table. Both MetCable executives, or such he now presumes as he tunes into their shop-talking badinage. Introductions are performed.

– You're what? Sod me. So he's managing director, Ralph, while you're chief executive and Pratt-face here is general manager. It seems to me you've got more pigging chiefs over there than Indians. Still, who's counting?

Edgar Bapty who will be joining us soon, he wants Jepcott to say, but Jepcott does not seem to be saying anything on those lines, to his slight consternation.

The two men are shown to the only remaining vacant table – yours. There are three chairs and so you do not have to move yet, but do note that Bapty is puzzling over something Jepcott has said about joining them for cheese and coffee and having a proper chat. In due course he sees what it is all about, as Jepcott unexpectedly rises and grips his hand, leaving Horner to look after him. It dawns on him that of the two supposed MetCable executives at your table, only the managing director is with MetCable, while the other, who was not properly identified to him, is almost certainly, like himself, a candidate for the appointment of contracts manager.

Jepcott is now crossing to your table. You will have to leave. Wait outside while Bapty and Horner finish their coffee. He should not be long: they do not seem to have much left to say to one another.

Has Edgar Samuel Bapty thought himself out of a job?

13

You'll get the blame for this. See if you don't.

His brain a bubbling stew of fury, frustration and disappointment, Bapty is nevertheless orderly enough in his mind to worry about first things first – the manner of his leaving.

– I really am cutting it a bit fine to get to that dental appointment, Peter. Look, I won't say good-bye to Ralph again as I can see he's tied up, but thanks again for a terrific meal, really enjoyed that – and – well, look forward to hearing from you. Ciao for now, eh?

That would have done very adequately had he said it, but he appears to have left in such a bluff flurry of overdone waggishness about his invented, aching tooth that he cannot remember what he did say, except that he has a sickening feeling it was quite plain to the entire restaurant that he is going nowhere near a dentist. He projects himself into a dentist's chair, opening wide, and feels indignant on his own behalf.

It is ten minutes to two as Bapty hurries towards the neighbourhood of the Law Courts from Covent Garden – Peel's proving to be just across the street from MetCable House was not only fortunate for you in being able to locate it so easily, it is also fortunate for Bapty in that it is quicker to walk than take a pig-driven cab, which would be bad for his indigestion. But on the corner of Drury Lane he comes to such an abrupt stop that a fellow-pedestrian close behind cannons into him. There is no time for the usual lengthy civil action for damages.

– Panjan*drums*.

Bapty is mortified. He hears himself, over lunch, tentatively letting go at the bureaucrats of the Independent Broadcasting

Authority – that seemed to go down well – but pronouncing them panjun*drams*. Not once, but twice. He sees Jepcott and Horner looking politely glassy-eyed while he double-somersaults into the pit.

Were there any other gaffes? He doesn't know. Setting off again almost at a jogtrot, he cannot move fast enough to get away from a stray recollection which the mispronounciation has thrown up. Inviting friends up in Bradthorpe to a Sunday lunchtime drinks party, his first ever, but calling it a soirée. Like snapshots filed away, he remembers the odd looks of people he no longer remembers, their features gone but their supercilious smiles remaining, like the Cheshire cat's grin.

– Ho Johnny no Johnny no-no-no-no-no
In an English country luggage bath;
Rimp-itty fildoh, lobby-gloddy bimbo. . . .

It has to be faced. Sweating rather, Bapty cross-examines himself.

Did he tell his Irish joke well? Was it too long, too *risqué*, offensive, not funny, the dialect awful?

Did he guffaw too long and loudly at the one Jepcott told, whatever might have been the point of it?

Did they notice his hand shake when he lit Jepcott's cigarette?

Should he have lit Jepcott's cigarette at all, fumbling with his stringy bookmatch when the supercilious bastard's own gold lighter could have carried out the task with a flick? Should he, like an over-attentive waiter, have at once passed over the ashtray?

Was he seen to bat dandruff off his shoulders?

When he snorted in simulated indignation at something he was expected to be indignant about – MetCable not getting all the tax concessions it felt entitled to or some such balls-aching whine – did a bubble of snot come down his nose?

Was he too servile, too casual, too cavalier, too urbane by half, too much the plain man, too cynical, too dull, too dim? Did they hear him fart? Did he, in sum, make a pratt of himself?

– Ho, no-ho John no.

Inconsequentially (as it would seem to anyone who has not been in Bapty's mind since before nine o'clock this morning) he transfers himself to a meeting of the Marine Estate Residents' Association into which he wandered drunk one evening and made some observations about dog shit on the pavements when he should have said dog dirt. His neighbours were shocked, though perhaps not so much as Bapty pretends (or fears: see how a remote anxiety cell in his head still houses a petition, yet to be organised, never mind delivered, demanding his removal from Portsea Sound). Arising out of his fancy that he is now ostracised throughout the neighbourhood, he homes in on the kernel of truth that feeds it – an encounter with the woman next door as she returns home with her shopping. An inconsequence within an inconsequence, he sees a big economy size drum of Saxa salt protruding from her bag. Embarrassed, they both simultaneously start to cross the street to avoid one another. It is left to Bapty to pretend that he has forgotten something and turn back. So put out was he – is he – at the inconvenience that this segment of memory has a statutory imagined coda: his neighbour treading in a dog turd as she reaches the sanctuary of the opposite pavement.

Lost in a maze of tangents, Bapty tries to find his way again, to marshal his thoughts. All he has to do is run the immediate past through like a video tape. But it's more difficult than it seems. Not for the first time today he worries about his inability to focus mentally; whereat he parades the excuses he usually puts forward: he has taken too much drink on board to concentrate properly, he is preoccupied by having a train to catch, he is too tired, he has to clear his mind of trivialities before he can get down to the essentials. At the back of this catalogue of justification he hears the voice of Dr Windows, now a neurology consultant, saying something about irreparable brain damage.

None of the standard excuses will fit the particular circumstances, which are that something has had the effect of disorienting Bapty, of so filling him with retroactive unease when he tries to summarise his impressions of the Jepcott lunch, that he cannot pull the necessary strings together. This something, he now reaches the conclusion, justifiably or not, as a sense of grievance wells up in his throat like gristle, is yourself. Or anyway, the sensation radiated by yourself, and not only during those few seconds in the lavatory. Did you, perhaps, linger by his table for a moment on your way out of the restaurant? Did you overhear him speaking to Horner? Bapty seems to think you did – seems to think, that is to say, that whatever influence it was that had the effect of paralysing his brain in the men's room, struck again during the last crucial moments over coffee, when he should have been craftily worming out of Horner his chances of joining MetCable. And not only then (though surely you would have been made aware of it if this were true) he goes on to claim that he was similarly afflicted on and off all through lunch. What he's probably doing here is exaggerating that one little frisson when he brushed past your table on his way to the phone, by way of excusing his disgraceful performance over lunch. But Bapty has got himself hopelessly confused now: he is mixing up whatever may be responsible for his inability to concentrate here and now with whatever was responsible for his inability to concentrate then and there. It all comes down to the same source, though. You get the blame.

You must not have this effect on Bapty. You must not have any effect on Bapty. It is against the rules of the game.

He can do it if he wants to, he succeeds in persuading himself as he hurries on towards the Aldwych. Those thoughts he has to marshal: all he has to do to shuffle them into place like so many dominoes is to count up to five. But not necessarily now. It's there on the mind-video, just waiting for him to slot it in and press the play button.

Chocolate. Passing the fancy sweet shop by the Waldorf Hotel Bapty throws the whole of his mind into thoughts of chocolate, this wave of hedonism bringing with it a sliver of anxiety that his occasional craving for a crafty Mars Bar could be a symptom of glucose deficiency, which in turn could be a symptom of *hairy spherical objects*. In his head he carries a vision of the perfect chocolate bar, shaped like a gold brick, all dark and solid, so dense that it has to be broken with a toffee hammer. He does not eat it: the gold brick chocolate bar, with its foil half stripped away, simply hangs in the air like a still life on a string, as it would in a classy advertisement placard.

One. Two. Three. Four. Five.

– *Once I caught a fish alive. Six, seven, eight nine ten, then I let it go again.*

Come along, Bapty. You can do it.

One. Two. Three. Four. Five. He hears Jepcott saying:

– Did have someone else in mind, but whether he's up to it or not remains to be—

No. Earlier than that. Wind the tape back more. Press the play button.

– Be frank with you, we're a new company, charting unexplored territory. For anyone looking for security we're not the best risk in the world.

Bapty hears himself replying oilily:

– After all, what is secure these days? No, I think the only consideration as regards that aspect for someone my age would be his pension situation, but that's my worry rather than MetCable's, isn't it?

That's what he actually said, the mind-initialled verbatim record. Now he plays back what he wanted to say, how he rephrased it to himself while Jepcott went on to make his next point.

– If we wanted security we'd be in the civil service, wouldn't we? No, if you're thinking about pension prospects, Ralph, the scheme Portsea Sound operate is so pathetic I did in fact have the nous good sense to drop out and make my own far better far superior far more beneficial arrangements, so there's there'd be no problem on that—

Bapty drifts off again. He's sitting in one of the tub chairs in the bow window of the Portsea Sailing Club with that sharp young man Yellowley, now established as an insurance broker. Bapty is studying, or affecting to study, the documents

Yellowley has laid before him, but the figures simply glaze over. He doesn't know what he is signing. Bapty is worried, but not on that score. Stroking his chin, he realises that his anxiety is that if the scheme proves to be so bogus or disadvantageous that he has no option but to turn it down, Yellowley will be disappointed. Yet he hardly knows the man.

Recognising, in a rare moment of insight, that wanting to please Yellowley springs from some deep-felt need to be nice once in a while, Bapty reflects ruefully that it would be cheaper to keep a dog. Banishing the thought as unconstructive, he then re-runs the whole pension scheme saga through again, but this time with Yellowley written out and Oliver Pease written in. They are playing golf – notice how Bapty's swing has improved since his last few holes about three hours ago.

– Do what your Uncle Edgar's done, laddie. Get yourself put on a contract basis, then persuade the buggers to give you a lump sum in lieu of their pension contributions and take out your own scheme. I can put you in touch with just the right man. Shit-hot, he is.

This is Bapty trying to convince himself he has made a shrewd deal, but fearing very much that he hasn't. Teeing off, he names a figure to Oliver, who whistles. Bapty, you will perceive, has two projected figures rattling about in his head: one merely doubling the Portsea Sound Company pension, the other more than quadrupling it – whether the minimum or the maximum sum put forward by Yellowley is uppermost in his mind depends less on the fluctuations of the unit trust market than on the fluctuations of Bapty's mood. Having, on this occasion, quoted the higher figure to Oliver he now scratches their game and quotes the lower figure to himself, adjusts it for broker's euphoria, and vainly tries to divide it by fifty-two to produce a weekly income. Jepcott comes to his rescue.

– In that case—

Rescue, that is, in the sense of a drowning man being thrown a brick. It's the key phrase coming up, Bapty tic-tacs to himself. The one that proves he made a total pratt of himself.

– In that case—

Big slabs of chocolate. Australia House. Glove spiked on railings. A bus. Another bus. Ho, ho-ho John no. St Clement Danes. Hi ho you two peh-hence say the bells of Saint Cle-heh-mens . . .

– In that case, and given that accommodation's no problem—

– Oh, no, as I say, I intend to sell the Portsea house anyway, added to which I shall need a base in London come what may—

– In that case, and if you seriously don't mean to renew your contract with Portsea—

Had he said that? Bapty whirrs the tape back further and hears himself saying it. Not, he recalls, to ingratiate or impress – it was simply a gesture, like the wave of a fat cigar, delivered in a fit of magnaminity. This was back in Jepcott's office, after Jepcott had invited Bapty to join him and Horner across at Peel's if he had nothing better to do. It was by way of reciprocation.

– Then let me suggest this. Why don't you try us for six months, no strings attached?

The record is blurred after that. Jepcott's voice rattles on but Bapty hears his own inner voice superimposed on it as he bitterly reproaches himself for woolgathering, for showing off, for allowing himself to be cornered like this.

– Oh, I don't think so, Ralph. I'm a bit too long in the tooth to do auditions.

– It's not a question of that, Edgar – is it, Peter? It's as much to see if we suit you as whether you suit us.

– I'd rather put it this way, Ralph. We'd both be taking a chance. You take a chance on me, I take a chance on you. Now do we back our own judgement or do we not. . . ?

It can be taken as read that you will not believe any of this. Even were you inclined to give Bapty the benefit of the doubt, his own voice running counterpoint to what he says he is saying there gives the game away:

– Oo, dear, I'd have to think about that, Ralph.

And Horner's voice coming in now:

– Then why don't we leave it like this . . . As Ralph has already indicated, we do have this other applicant to see . . .

Bapty recalls the regret surging into his mind at that point: not so much at the possibility of not landing the job as of no longer having an excuse enough to allow himself some long-promised and keenly-anticipated indulgence. He produces it, a dog-eared souvenir snapshot of the postulated future, and studies it wistfully. He is in a club of some kind. There are people all around him shaking his hand, and he is getting in a large order of drinks. Evidently one of his haunts – you have not seen this place before. Nor, since the events you are watching are now unlikely to take place, is it necessarily on the cards that you will be seeing it in due course.

What was said next? Something about no tearing hurry and thinking it over. He racks his brains but it's like raking the ashes of a dead fire. He doesn't know, that's the top and bottom of it. Has he left it that he'll think it over or that they'll think it over? He doesn't know. He was too busy thinking.

He has bungled it for sure. He has bungled it so much that he doesn't know whether he has bungled it or not.

Bapty, aware that he has been walking too fast, stops where the Strand meets Fleet Street, clutching his racing heart. He breathes in deeply. To Dr Windows, who has not opened his mouth, he utters *Bollocks*, and deliberately, as if choosing a greetings card or some other item of merchandise from a revolving rack, goes about selecting a subject to last him out the remainder of his journey from the following display:

Climbing into bed with Margot after lunch (but instantly relegated into reserve on the objection *but not being able to get it up*).

Taking Ruth on the Portsea Ferry to Dieppe. Pipedream cancelled: the gonorrheal twat-faced slime-brained pillocking seamen are on strike.

Chocolate.

His obituary, as it might appear in some unspecified newspaper. Bapty keeps this on file in his head, from time to time updating it . . . *In the last year of his life Bapty was successfully engaged in a series of altercations with the British Rail staff at Portsea Station . . .* But not now. Not in the mood.

His mother. No – too fraught, as a quick preview tells him:

– That's a funny carry-on, then. So they've not told you whether you've got the job or not?

– No, you see they've other people to see, interview.

– Still, you must have a good chance. They must think highly of you, to take you out to a restaurong.

A poison-pen letter to the woman next door.

Standing over a ratty little graffitist with a shotgun while he scrubs PORTSEA RANGERS ARE A BUNCH OF SHIT off the sea wall.

Catching Margot out.

Yes – he'll settle for that one, despite his awareness that having Margot playing the lead will bring in an undertow of anxiety at being late for his second lunch, while his own role – involving as it does a change of job – is bound to contain disturbing echoes of the lunch he's just had. So it won't be entirely escapist. It's one of his favourites, though.

He's working for one of the big television companies in London, the BBC probably, and he's been in the United States looking at satellite developments. He's called Margot from the airport to say he's about to catch his plane home – but what the stupid fornicating bitch doesn't know is that the airport he's at is Heathrow, not Kennedy. He takes a cab to Viceroy Court, to his flat of the future he wishes they'd once lived in, and sees the light burning in the bedroom window, which for present purposes is on the sixth floor. Now he's about to catch her redhanded. He won't do anything melodramatic. He'll just open the window and throw all the man's clothes down into Gloucester Road. Then:

– Do you want to follow them, or would you prefer to go out by the door?

There's a good deal more of this. He doesn't reproach Margot, doesn't say anything at all, just treats her with cunningly weary resignation. Until she is driven to say:

– Look, Sam. We can't go on like this . . .

A letter falls into Bapty's head, as through a mail slot. *Dear Edgar, Peter Horner and I very much enjoyed our lunch with you the other day. Thank you for giving us your time. I think you will probably have formed the view that Metropolitan Cable is not for you at this stage in your career, and in my view you have made a wise decision.*

There is another one by the same post. *Dear Edgar, Peter Horner and I very much enjoyed our lunch with you today. Alan will be writing to you formally in a few days, but this is just to say at once that we should be delighted to have you on board. If you will confirm that you are still available and willing, we can get down to the . . .*

Which one is the forgery? For the moment, Bapty neither knows nor cares. He is with Margot again. Unwisely, and despite his warning to himself, he has after all taken up his option on the very first of the selection of thought-subjects on offer, and is now lying moodily beside her, thinking *Cowbag* and saying:

– Well, I screwed that one, didn't I?

– You didn't screw me, though, did you?

Is that how Margot talks? We shall see.

– You drink too much, Sam, that's your trouble.

Is she saying that? – in other words, has she ever said that? – or is he making her say it? It's difficult to know whether Bapty is putting words into her mouth or whether this is the kind of thing you can expect of Margot should he succeed (the prospect seems remote) in getting her into bed after two lunches.

A twinge of pain as he turns into Buffs Court. Not indigestion yet, but the threat of it.

– You did *what*?

That's the incredulous voice of Dr Windows, over a Sunday morning sherry at the bar of the Sailing Club.

– I had two lunches.

Dr Windows, in mock exasperation, turns to his companions – most of the staff of Portsea Sound.

– And I'm supposed to be his medical adviser! It's like being safety officer on the *Titanic*!

A barrister walking up Buffs Court turns and stares at Bapty as, soundlessly chuckling, he crossed the threshold of Mrs Grundy's.

14

So this is the famous Margot, then. In the flesh. She is not at all what you have been expecting.

Perhaps she keeps her sluttishness for the bedroom. That trail of crumpled Kleenex and those dabs of cotton wool, the strewn clothes, the overflowing ashtrays you see every time he has the pair of them alone together, it's all too vivid not to be true. Exaggerated possibly – Bapty's capable of fixing on some minor slovenly manifestation like leaving spilled face powder on the dressing table, and blowing it up out of all proportion. Or perhaps it's all in the mind. Hers, that is, not his. If, as he believes, she has the moral mentality of a slut, he may have adorned her with the manners of one, a kind of branding so that the teeming population of his head will know her for what she is.

She's not bad looking. Lost some weight since you first caught a back view of her, the day Bapty tracked her down to that Berkeley Square mews. That was a good few years ago, of course. Going on forty by now, he has her down as, but you would guess nearer thirty. Worn well, considering her supposed record. Black suit again – it seems to be her colour – and white high-necked jumper; dark glasses pushed up over long dark hair. A business outfit, but not so businesslike that it doesn't know the effect it is making. Margot is dressed, indeed, as if expecting to meet someone special. Not Bapty, he acknowledges at once as he sights her from the doorway: she wouldn't have had time to go home and change. Who, then? He wonders, coming towards her, if she has stood up a lunch date or alternatively is meeting someone for cocktails later this afternoon. On the answer will depend whether Bapty will be flattered or fall into a mental sulk. He opts for flattery: she was supposed to be having a clandestine lunch with whoever her flavour of the month happens to be, but she has put him off.

Mrs Grundy's certainly does have a clandestine lunching air about it. Occupying a warren of old whitewashed brick cellars, its dining area is a series of vaulted alcoves, each housing one candle-lit table. It being past two o'clock by now, the tables that have been vacated already are unlikely to be reoccupied. The vacant alcove across the paved central space from Margot's should do you very nicely.

Bapty stoops and kisses her lightly on the lips, thinking *Same* at the touch of them. Half-rising, she raises a hand to brush his cheek. He thinks again, *Same*.

They are evidently on better terms in this surface real life than they are in the real real life within the closed retreat of Bapty's cranium. There are two glasses on the table. Gin and tonic, hers looks like. A dry sherry for him. A nice touch, to have remembered and arranged to have it waiting, you might think, but not Bapty. He has already recovered from what he now regards as his pitifully weak exhibition of marshmallow sentimentality at the remembered contact. Raising his glass in salute, what he does think is:

– Cheap gestures don't cost much, do they, my darling?

Delivered with what he imagines is a Noël Coward air, it is manifestly not a line he has just made up, for it is not really appropriate to the occasion – especially if she is paying for the drinks. Obviously it is one of a ready-made range he keeps in stock, a reach-me-down retort for a variety of situations.

Bapty takes in his surroundings at a glance and revises his notes for *The Good Food Guide*:

– Mrs Grundy's, Buffs Court, EC4. Lamb dressed as mutton. Expensive fake ye olde dyve only one up from a wine bar, where Fleet Street hackettes and hacks pay through the nose not to be seen . . .

– You tosspotting bloody cowbag – come on, then, how many have there been?

Leaving his *Good Food Guide* write-up aside for the time

being, Bapty puts the question without rancour and even quite genially, his mind not expecting to be furnished with an answer nor even very much concerned with the question, which appears as routine as it is rhetorical. What really concerns Bapty's mind is *Who else has she been here with?* He sees her at this very table, hands locked across it with, for want of any more recent candidate he is able to bring to mind, the Portsea Sound managing director Lance Barrington.

It is old Henry, wandering across drink in hand as if Mrs Grundy's were the wine bar Bapty has condemned it as being only one up from, who tells him what he wants to know yet wants not to know.

– Who else has she *not* been here with, old boy, that's what you ought to be asking yourself unless you're just trying to kill time. You do know they draw lots in Fleet Street to decide who's going to have her next? I'll tell you what, old man, you're well rid of the two-timing little bitch, if you don't mind my saying so.

Bapty does mind him saying so and feels bitterly resentful, but he can't be rude to old Henry, not to his face. Instead he sends him an anonymous letter. *If you weren't such a self-opinionated pompous pratt, you might have some inkling what a pigging bore everyone finds you . . .* He'll see that it never reaches Henry, though. He has too much of a soft spot for the old bugger.

Avoid the leaden quiche starter he appends to the *Good Food Guide* entry, then commences a violent quarrel with the waitress who has just gone into the kitchen over her refusal to serve him a plain boiled egg. The noise you can hear reverberating through his head, like the beat of a bass drum, is Bapty suppressing an attack of hiccoughs. He tries to frighten them away – *I have your X-rays here, Mr Bapty. I'm sorry to have to tell you it's a sarcoma of the jaw* – but to no avail. He really has got indigestion now. There is nothing on this menu he can possibly eat and feel well after it.

– Sorry to have buggered you about, darling – I got here as quickly as I could but I seem to be running late today.

– You're not to run at all, Sam – especially on my account. You know what Dr Killjoy says.

– Bugger Dr Killjoy.

– Do you think he'd like that? Besides, what's happened to your spherical objects?

– Alive and well and dangling in their usual position.

Underneath these banalities and innuendos, faintly, you may detect the notes he is making of – or preparing for – the conversation that is going on in actuality – the *how are you after all this time?* and *I must say you're looking well* type of pleasantry, friendly enough but well this side of intimacy. Dr Killjoy, of course, is the joke name, invented by Bapty to put in the mouth of Margot, for the man who has just pronounced the fatal diagnosis on his jaw.

Margot appears to have much to say, though of little consequence judging by the sample soundings taken by Bapty. Under cover of her prattle he now proposes to hold his breath and count his hiccoughs. Whatever number he has arrived at when the attack stops will be the number of lovers Margot has had since they last met.

While counting, he strips her naked, shackles her, spreadeagled, across the table and stimulates her to the point at which she is shrieking to be raped, whereupon he raises the trilby hat he has borrowed from Henry the better to play out this charade, and bids her good afternoon.

Thirty-three. Bapty calls that an under-estimate but it seems to have done the trick, and in any case any further advance is forestalled by the requirement upon him to speak.

– Oh, just passing through keeping in touch seeing a few old faces been to the – most – *boring* conference had to see the quack routine check-up senior management seminar thought I'd give myself a day off for a change . . .

Whichever explanation for his presence in London he may be offering, it is significant that he does not mention his interview with Metropolitan Cable. He does, however, receive Margot's scornful reaction to this confidence:

– You must be out of your tiny Chinese. MetCable are just

about the last word in television, ducky – what on earth would they want with a third-rate old has-been from steam radio?

Studying the menu he wonders if she ever talks about him. Did his first wife Pam used to talk about him? More to the point, does she still? He sees Juney confiding in the plumber who has come to attend to her clogged-up wastepipe. If Bapty's three wives have discussed him with only three friends or companions each, and those three have each retailed the confidences to three more, then that would be three times three times three equals twenty seven plus the three wives plus the nine original confidantes equals . . . And that, Bapty persuades himself, is only the tip of the iceberg. Staring intently at the item *Chicken casserole* until the letters re-form themselves into *Chicken arsehole*, he conducts such a prodigious census of the tittle-tattles and rumour-mongers breeding like field-mice in his head that by the time he has determined on another steak for lunch they fill the Albert Hall, with a convoy of luxury coaches down from Glassborough stretching all the way into Knightsbridge.

Another steak is a ludicrous choice. Bapty justifies it by telling himself that if the steak he ate at Peel's had been twice as big, and he had eaten all of it as he would have felt obliged to have done to avoid offending his hosts, then it would have been no more than the steak he ordered there plus the steak he is about to order here; or conversely, the steak he is about to consume here plus the steak he has already consumed there amount to no more than if he hadn't eaten the first steak but the second were double the size. In short, he is not devouring two lunches, he is devouring one lunch spread over two restaurants.

Wine arrives. Margot and Bapty toast one another, clinking glasses. He observes, still without rancour:

– You bloody near destroyed me, Margot, do you know that?

See him, as he thinks this thought, bare his uneven, yellow teeth in laughter at some reminiscence. They are talking about old times. Bapty riffles through his catalogue of pleasant or at least relatively innocuous memories and associations touching on Margot, a slim companion volume to the one he usually consults in connection with her, and plumps for an elaborate and shapeless anecdote to do with wallpapering their first flat, the one that figures in Bapty's mind as more garret-like and bohemian than perhaps it was, and which as he develops this saga of their earlier and, by inference, happier days, now appears as an absurdly small yet immensely cosy love-nest that might have been designed for a television comedy series about two penniless newlyweds.

The lunch proceeds amicably. Bapty plods contentedly through a steak even bigger than the one he finished not half an hour ago, his initial alarmed eructation of acids at the sight of it transmuted effortlessly into saliva. A second carafe of wine appears. He is feeling so benign that he withdraws, un-reservedly, any criticism he may have made of the staff's unparalleled incompetence and instead recommends them jointly for the Waitress of the Year award. Jepcott intervenes seldom, Dr Windows not at all. The conversation, all of it seemingly on a personal level, flows easily from sub-topic to sub-topic. They are discussing Margot's career now. Out of each set of appropriate compliments or laudatory interjections he places before himself for consideration, Bapty invariably selects the most fawning. He is searching for a way of telling her how much he misses her without it sounding like a whine when suddenly Margot stabs him with her steak knife.

Or such it feels like, as Bapty drops his fork in shock. The pain in his chest is excruciating. It is not indigestion, for that is a separate, duller ache in a different region. It is not his heart. It is Margot. She has said something.

Wait for the replay. Wait for Bapty's stalled brain to mesh back into gear.

Margot has broken some quite important news. *By the way, Sam, I don't know whether it's reached Portsea yet, but I've been invited to become an honest woman again and I've said I'll think about it, in fact I've said yes.*

No articulate feedback yet. Having first recorded he is now

re-recording her exact words over and over at ever-increasing speeds until on the tenth or eleventh re-run they sound like animated-cartoon gabble – *By the way, Sam, don't know wibble-blibble pibble ibble wibble gibble sibble thibble yes.* They will remain in his head, he knows, for all time, like Alan Twentyman's nose-picking admonition. It would need a prefrontal leucotomy to erase one syllable.

At even more terrific speeds now, so fast that not one word in fifty is picked up and transmitted to his consciousness in anything like verbally recognisable form, dozens of possible responses recommend themselves to Bapty. Out of a flashed spectrum of reactions ranging from blank disbelief to a disjointed promise to kill himself, his mind is so sludge-witted that it can pull in only the slowest and lamest: *Well well well well well.*

It has simply not occurred to Bapty – not, anyway, today, during the period to which you have had access, when assuredly it has not occurred to you either – that she would do such a thing. He has not even explicitly acknowledged her legal right to do it. Divorce, you will have noticed, is not a subject that has occupied Bapty's mind for one instant today. Pam, Juney and Margot have appeared not in their present roles of former wives, but in their former roles of present wives. It has been apparent too that although various courts have claimed his attendance in one capacity or another today – the crown court, as witness against the Portsea railway clerk who technically stole his Access card, the juvenile court to which he was summoned as a prosecution witness against the small girl who dropped the chocolate wrapper, the law courts where he sought exemplary damages against the van driver who blew his horn at him as he was crossing Gloucester Road this morning – the divorce court, in which he must have been something of a regular in real life, has seen nothing of him. Nor does it now: but Bapty does at least, and at last, briefly recognise, by way of formalising the arrangement she has just announced, that documents do exist entitling the last of the former Mrs Baptys to take this step.

His mental visibility improving somewhat as the daze he is in thins to a half-daze, Bapty next applies himself to the task of vocalising a response for Margot's consumption. He prepares a batch of possibles with the speed and dexterity of a master baker turning out bread rolls:

– You never!

– Well well well well well.

– Do you know, I had a funny feeling you were going to say that.

– Tell me, what's the etiquette in these matters? Is the ex-husband supposed to get stung for a prezzie?

– Oh, yes, and I suppose you want me to give you away?

– You never know, Margot, I might yet beat you to it.

– Does the poor sod know what he's letting himself in for?

– I'm very happy for you, Margot. I mean that.

– Really? Who's the lucky man?

Patently it is the last of these options to which he chooses to give voice, for the neurons and synapses of the pulsating lump of tissue that is the brain of Edgar Samuel Bapty are already processing her answer.

It does not make sense.

Margot has told Bapty, or Bapty's mind alleges that Margot has told Bapty, that she intends to marry his saloon bar crony Henry.

How can Margot marry a figment of Bapty's imagination?

She cannot, of course. It follows, then, either that she does not mean to marry Henry, or that she does and Henry is not after all imaginary.

Albemarle. The word splatters into Bapty's mind like a hurled egg. What can he mean? Is it one of his hysteria-induced nonsense concoctions, like *Luggage bath*?

Henry is not after all imaginary. You have it on the authority of *The Times* as Bapty savagely frames the announcement. *The marriage has been arranged and will shortly take place between Henry pig-pissing rat-faced bollock-festering swining Albermarle and Mrs Margot Bapty (nee Cowbag).*

It must come as news to you that Henry has a surname – that Henry turns out to be his real forename, even, for it was only a sketchy impression, as he himself was. Now that shadowy yet substantial apparition turns to flesh before your eyes, the creased check suit filling out like a blown-up tyre, the tankard-clutching hand becoming mapped with veins, silver hair sprouting like a transplant beneath the trilby hat. Only his features remain vague, suggesting that Bapty does not know his old friend very well. But Henry lives all right.

The red mist undulates through Bapty's head like the swirling vapours of the universe at the beginning of Creation. A world is forming. Henry, the victim, it would seem, of an audacious bodysnatching operation whereby his physical corpus was forcibly donated to the creature brought to life in the laboratory of Bapty's mind, is to be restored to his rightful personality.

The picture jigsaws together as Margot talks and Bapty listens, feeding such nuggets of information as he regards as salient to that department of his brain now as assiduously engaged as the staff of the Great Soviet Encyclopedia in hastily reassessing Henry Albemarle from harmless drinking companion to two-timing old lecher.

Something about the novel Margot is writing, or says she is writing – Bapty puts ironic inverted commas round the claim . . . advice from Henry . . . contacts . . . knows all the publishers . . . *Went on from there, did it? I'm sure it pigging went on from there* . . . found herself in next office to him after re-joining paper . . . shoulder to cry on . . . *Yes, I can imagine. I bet you both cried all the way back to bed, didn't you?*

Henry seems to work on the same paper . . . books editor, would he be? Should have been made features editor . . . passed over . . . more talent in his little finger than . . . *You didn't talk like that when I was pigging passed over at Thames pigging Radio time after pigging time, did you? Oh, no, it was because I was such a stick-in-the-mud. Well I'll tell you one thing, you little cowbag. If I'm a stick-in-the-mud, that pratt qualifies as a fucking hippopotamus. I mean Henry, for*

Christ's sake! Or are you going to call him something differ-
ent, like you did me? How about Ringo?

He is a man of no little resilience, this Bapty. Already he is
making the best of it. You have seen him able to half-persuade
himself that while that Berkeley Square mews photographer
may well have seduced Margot, he cannot have seduced her
very much since he is either a homosexual or next door to a
eunuch. Now, and on firmer ground here given Henry's
undisputed age – he comes out as a good five years Bapty's
senior – he has little difficulty in convincing himself that
Margot's future husband will be little more than a platonic
companion, a silly, cuckolded old man dozing by the fireside
while his wife flits wantonly from one brief affair to the next,
barely bothering to cover her tracks – she even lets her young
gigolos pick her up at the flat, house, country pigging cottage
or wherever they will be living.

He is glad she is marrying Henry. It will prevent her
marrying someone else – almost certainly a young stud with
whom she would have been at it like knives all night long
instead of, according to the set-up Bapty has planned for her,
having to turn celibate by midnight like a sexual Cinderella.

But now Bapty is sick of Henry. He has had Henry all
through the remainder of his steak, not a morsel of which has
gone uneaten though a dew of sweat still sits on his brow at the
effort of it, and now Henry is trespassing on the small piece of
Brie he has decided to allow himself to keep Margot company.
He blames Henry for the flatulence that is causing him to
concentrate all his being on stifling a belch when he ought to be
engaged on rapidly ageing Margot by about twenty years, to
make her so raddled and with any luck diseased that no-one
will look at her.

The carafe is empty again. For the second time today Bapty
announces:

– Well, I think champagne is called for, wouldn't you say?

This echo of his previous lunch at Peel's brings into Bapty's
mind the isolated, ice-clear realisation that if Ralph Jepcott
turns him down – as almost certainly he already effectively has

131

done – then he is stuck at Portsea Sound until retirement. But he has no time to dwell on that just now. There are more important fish to fry.

– All right, now you were working on that swining book before we left London – when we agreed to make a fresh start. Was the bugger advising you then? Is that what you were doing when you used to come up from Portsea once a week twice a week every chance you could get, to 'keep in touch' as you put it? We know just who you were keeping in touch with now, don't we?

Bapty has ordered not champagne but large Armagnacs – a drink that has strong associations for him and Margot, judging by the amount of it he has already taken with her in spirit today – together with the large cigar he has been promising himself, though not a celebratory one in all the circumstances. As he lights it with his Peel's restaurant bookmatch, he has her fondly remonstrating with him:

– Oh, Sam, now how am I to believe you're looking after yourself when you're still smoking like a chimney?

To which Bapty retorts:

– Freckled spherical objects.

But not, surprisingly, to Dr Windows, who does not put in an appearance here. It is to Margot – to whom he continues in tones of resigned exasperation:

– So while I was perjuring myself to your pigging solicitors to give you the divorce you were on your knees begging for, all the time you were getting yourself advised rotten by that geriatric pratt Henry Albemarle!

But he no longer has the steam to make it sound as if any of this matters. The truth is that Bapty is rapidly losing interest in his rhetorical interrogation as two far more attractive themes commend themselves in succeeding flashes of inspiration. The first is:

– I don't suppose there's any chance of one last roll in the sack for the sake of Auld Lang Syne, is there?

And the second:

– RING RUTH.

15

It is 3.45, or as Bapty's mind would have it, 3.25. He enters the Charing Cross Road branch of his bank yet does not enter it for it is closed, but several important transactions do take place.

It is fortunate that you were able to keep tabs on his movements – that when Margot, en route for her next assignment (or assignation, if you are to believe Bapty), offered him a lift in the radio cab that collected her at Mrs Grundy's, he ran through the request *If I ask you to drop me at Cambridge Circus, you won't assume I'm going to rot the afternoon away at the Broadcasters Club, will you?* to himself before voicing it or its equivalent to her.

You have caught up with him just as, the cab having decanted him hard by the bank, he simultaneously pens a letter to its manager while with the same hand waving Margot on her way. It will be interesting to learn, in due course, whether there were any significant developments in Bapty's head during the taxi ride. Very likely, having managed to get through to Ruth while at Mrs Grundy's and being full of her during that last coffee and Armagnac, he will have been full of her still.

Who is the enigma that is Ruth? You have seen her tranquil face often enough, but learned nothing about her. Returning from successfully telephoning her, he said little to himself about her that could lend itself to intelligent interpretation, but simply retained her in his mind's eye like a miniature in a locket, feasting on her wistful smile and faraway-looking eyes, and keening *Ruth, Ruth* as is his wont. Has he arranged to see her today? His mind did not say. No more, however, was heard of his fanciful scheme to bed Margot one last time. That may be significant.

– Dear Sir, I have had an account with your bank at various branches originally in Bradthorpe and Glassborough and latterly in London and Portsea, over a period of thirty years. During this period all this time I have never been overdrawn except by arrangement . . .

It is plain that the letter has no point or purpose. Bapty has no complaint against his bank. The opening paragraph is one that he has stored in readiness, as in a word-processor, against any grievance that may come along. That is what he is doing in the bank outside of opening hours. He is looking for one.

Crossing Cambridge Circus he is writing the cheque he has just made a mental note to cash at the Broadcasters Club, having forgotten to go to the bank earlier, while at the same time collecting Italian currency and traveller's cheques for his honeymoon with Margot.

– When you say I'm allowed only to take fifty poundsworth eighty poundsworth sixty poundsworth of lire in currency into the country, are you telling me that your bank is subject to Italian law, then, or what? No, no, no, I'm just trying to establish what my possible future transgressions while going through the Venice customs have got to do with you. Perhaps they've got an account with you . . . You see, the claim you appear to be making is that if it should happen to be against Islamic law, let's say, to import more than fifty poundsworth of shekels or whatever they deal in, and I want a hundred poundsworth, it's your bounden duty to cut my right hand off.

First round to Bapty. One of his standards, by the sound of it.

Striding purposefully along Charing Cross Road he now moves to another counter where he presents his cheque:

– You have my signature on the cheque. You have my signature on the bank card. Why do you now wish my signature on the back of the cheque? I see. Any other cross-check you'd like to make? My driving licence perhaps? Passport? Birth certificate?

The bank set is dismantled. Bapty's personal scene shifter now rapidly constructs a coroner's court. The coroner, or the grizzled character actor Bapty has cast as coroner – probably someone he has seen in a film or on a bus – is examining a letter as he addresses the jury:

– This is altogether extraordinary, members of the jury. I will read the note and you must make of it what you will. 'To whom it may concern. This afternoon, at approximately 3.25, I went into the Charing Cross Road branch of my bank to cash a cheque. The cashier was so unhelpful, unpleasant and objectionable that, still upset some five hours later, I have decided to take my life . . .'

All this self-indulgence has a purpose. Bapty is keeping something from himself. By picking quarrels with innocent bank tellers and swaying inquest juries in his favour, he hopes to hold some less agreeable subject at bay.

Margot's wedding, could it be? Something to do with Margot, for she is forcing herself back into his consciousness with the lock-proof remorselessness of a ghost intent on haunting.

All Bapty's whistling in the dark is in vain. Back he is with her in her cab. He has taken her hand. Or she has taken his. Both versions present themselves for Bapty's approval – the first must be the authentic one, you will probably conclude, not being inclined to give our hero the benefit of the doubt. It is not necessarily so. She seems an affectionate creature (Bapty would not argue with that) and it may be the kind of impetuous thing she would do, perhaps feeling a little sorry for an ex-husband who from time to time looks so careworn and crumpled in his dandruff-speckled too-tight dark blue velvet suit that he could be a provincial dance-band leader whom time has seen off. At any rate, they are holding hands, or Margot is suffering her hand to be held: upon which Bapty feels emboldened to think:

– So what do you say to one more time? By way of burying the hatchet or should I say the chopper?

Bapty cringes at his own rhinocerous-hide indelicacy. There

are probably other stabs at the question, of a greater or lesser degree of coarseness, but he is permitted to feel that he has punished himself enough on this one. He moves on to the next stage:

– Tell him you're on a job. After all, if you change switch substitute the definite article for the indefinite, it'd be no more than the truth, now would it?

To this he adds, *And it's what you always used to tell me, you cowbag, isn't it?* – but this is strictly an aside for his own consumption only. It is somewhat pernickety of Bapty to insist on this distinction, for when all's said and done, he is doing no more all along, as he turns off Charing Cross Road along one of the alleys leading into Soho, than confining within his head what has gone no further than his head in the first place. Or so it is to be hoped. If he said anything remotely on those lines to Margot he will have got short shrift, if her tongue is half as sharp as the one attributed to her by Bapty. Could that be the cause of his wincing embarrassment as he recalls these crude overtures? Unlikely: for her reply would have been of the order that gets etched in his memory with acid – whereas the only response he puts on record is of her smiling and patting his hand, after the manner of a flattered woman of the world gently letting down a gauche and precocious suitor.

– You wouldn't have to come back to the bungalow, I know how you hate have always hated always hated the place. It would put me off seeing you being put off would put me off knowing you were put off, if you see what I mean. No, we could always stay at the Majestic.

It has to be said for Bapty's mind that it does not do things by halves. Turning up out of the blue after two years, not only is he proposing that his former wife mark her impending re-marriage by indulging him in one last fling, but he now puts it to her that she might like to trail down to Portsea for the privilege of so accommodating him. Chance would be a fine thing, Bapty.

– I could book us in through Portsea Sound – the Majestic's under new management complete change of staff since you were down perfectly discreet they know me there don't know me from Adam wouldn't know you from Eve. Mr and Mrs Smith or whoever – come down to do a programme, haven't we . . . ?

The Awkward Squad, or perhaps Speaking Freely, would that be? Bapty shrugs it all off. He has done with the whole sordid episode now. He has got it out of his system. It is plain now why he went to such lengths to blot it out of his consciousness. In Bapty's own words, as he closes the book on his cab-ride with Margot, he made a total pratt of himself.

The Broadcasters Club. One of those narrow Soho doorways leading up a flight of steep, worn-lino stairs into the previous mind of E. S. Bapty, as he here signs himself in. You have been here before, briefly, as legitimate a member's guest then as you are now. It is where Bapty held his little celebration upon winning his MetCable appointment.

Few of the members you saw then are here now. Of those who are here, only one or two appear to know Bapty, and that slightly. Stripped of its bonhomie, it is a cheerless, barrack-like room that you see – an off-peach plastic quilted bar, a few pub tables and chairs and a fruit machine make up the furnishings. Crossing the lino floor, Bapty exchanges nods with the couple of members who recognise him, his nod more cordial than theirs. He greets one of the convivial group of three clustered at the bar, hoping to be drawn into their company by the offer of a drink which he may then reciprocate.

– That's very kind of you, Frank. Now what shall I have? Let me see, oh, better make it a beer this time of day . . .

His prospective host half-smiles vaguely and turns back to his companions, making a show of being deep in private conversation.

– You snot-snivelling pratt.

Bapty orders himself the beer he has just asked for – a half pint. He is wise. Although he is not yet drunk, he has taken a fair quantity on board today what with one thing and another, and it is time to pace himself. Plainly, Bapty can drink a good deal without it going to his head (which equally plainly has no need of stimulants), but it does not require Dr Windows to tell him he is doing himself no good. The cigar he has been smoking has left him short of breath – he inhales as one would a cigarette: no wonder he anxiously reproves himself through the agency of Margot – and his digestive system is still uttering protests at his treatment of it.

The barman, having served his beer, reaches down a drum of panatellas. Bapty takes a handful. He is on the slippery slope now.

– You misheard me, my friend. I didn't ask if I *could* cash a cheque, I said I would *like* to cash a cheque. However, should you wish to make an issue out of it, there are enough of us here to make a form a quorum, so supposing we call an extraordinary general meeting and put it to the test . . .

The transaction having gone through without demur, Bapty lights a panatella and looks around the room, fixing on the pencil-moustached, sleek-haired figure in blazer and gaberdine slacks who is playing the fruit machine.

You have no way of knowing how much or how little the Broadcasters Club is used by broadcasters, but certainly the man at the fruit machine, who has the looks and the air of a thirties film star, is well known to you as a radio personality with his own morning chat show. He is a friend or at least an acquaintance of Bapty's – or at least so Bapty claims, producing as evidence authentic footage of a sociable afternoon at this very bar, when Bapty and the celebrity were among a crowd of a dozen or so exchanging jokes and banter. Slowing the track down, Bapty proves that this household name spoke to him directly at least twice, once very nicely to refuse a drink, the other to remark *I believe you* in response to some now extinct observation of Bapty's.

Those strange twitching grimaces, reminiscent of the traumatic nervous spasms of the little girl he had locked up for dropping litter, represent Bapty's attempts to catch the famous man's eye.

– Rollo. How are you?

Rollo (to emulate Bapty's familiarity) cannot help but have

noticed Bapty's arrival in the sparsely-occupied club, but he has so far shown no sign of recognition. Now Bapty, glass poised in readiness, wills him to glance in his direction. As if in hypnotic submission he does chance to do so, upon which Bapty ostentatiously raises the glass in salutation. The celebrity, apprehending a complete stranger wishing to ingratiate himself into his company, gives the briefest of nods and in his desperation to avoid the encounter achieves the paradoxical impossibility of sauntering hastily across the room to join a colleague or friend.

– Oh, yes, known him for years. Knew him when his shirt lap was hanging out, as we used to say up in Bradthorpe Glassborough my part of the world drink with him many times old days perfectly nice bloke but it's the usual story, success gone to his—

His heart is not in this: too mild by far. Even if it were not, no mere character assassination is adequate enough to accommodate Bapty's burning hatred at the snub he has received. He prepares a revenge so fiendishly sickening that his mind at once censors it, as he knew it would, hence the innocuous substitute that preceded it. Bapty wholly capitulates, not only allowing the culprit to escape scot free but actually bragging to Ralph Jepcott over drinks in the latter's office, *By the way, no sooner had I left you come out of the dentist that day than I bumped into a very old mutual friend of ours . . .* He breaks off, more nauseated even than at what has just been going on in the League of Justice's torture cellar.

The scene changes from the Broadcasters Club now to the Broadcasters Club on some future occasion. It is crowded with the denizens of Bapty's cancelled MetCable jamboree.

– Heard about Edgar Bapty?
– No, what?
– Dead.
– You're joking!
– Strong smell of gas, so the story goes. I don't know the full details but apparently he had some steaming row with that big-headed berk Rollo. You know how he let things build

up and get on top of him and that must have been the last straw . . .

Honour tortuously satisfied, Bapty drains his beer and orders another, at the same time issuing the memo *Pee before leaving*. Reference to leaving prompts him to consult his watch, but the action yields no comment. He thinks of crossing to talk to the one person in the club who has had the grace to nod to him without also making it clear that the salute is to be regarded as the beginning and end of their social transactions, but decides instead to talk to a man who has just gone out, whom he also knows slightly.

– Oh, just looking around, you know, doing a bit of chinwagging here and there. No, as a matter of fact I'm in grave danger of being sucked into all this cable and satellite how's-your-father some tempting offers very tempting indeed but means upping sticks and moving back to London who needs it? Added to which, at the speed rate pace things are moving happening at Portsea Sound I'd be pretty stupid in many ways to move pack it in at this stage of the game. Oh, yes, it's all happening all go. You do know we've put in for the new television franchise if it ever comes about bound to quite on the cards touch wood . . .

There seems little else to be said about Bapty's career prospects. Allowing the monologue to wind down like an old gramophone he looks at his watch again, this time registering that it wants sixteen minutes to the hour of 4.28. *Ruth*. It is a curiously precise time to be setting off to meet anyone, as his mind-planner is insisting that he must. Perhaps he is allowing an exact half hour, say, for a particular train he has to catch; or perhaps they have a regular rendezvous somewhere and he knows from experience that it will take just seventeen minutes to keep his 4.45 appointment or it could be thirty-two minutes to keep a five o'clock one. It would help if Bapty would reveal where Ruth is to be found. You could have your work cut out to keep track of him this time.

There is, mark you, no guarantee that it is indeed Ruth he plans on setting out to meet. He has yet to disclose it in so many words, and the fact that she flashed into his mind coincidentally with the reminder to leave at 4.28 signifies little. She wanders in and out like a domestic cat, this Ruth.

Wait. As luck would have it he is meeting her this second . . . but for lunch, two hours ago, at Mrs Grundy's. Once again he has her usurping Margot, a cuckoo now rather than a cat.

It is pretty well the scene as he had it soon after arranging the venue with Margot this morning, though with the imagined actual restaurant now replacing the imagined imaginary one, and with Ruth's sad and sensual expression attached to her own face rather than, as then, grafted on the host-physiognomy of Margot. Otherwise it is all too familiar: the Armagnac, the yearning, the hands held across the table . . . Yes, it is old stuff, this.

By the way, Sam, I don't know whether it's reached Portsea yet, but I've been invited to become an honest woman again . . .

Poor Bapty, to have more ghosts walking his head than are be found in the whole works of Shakespeare. And just when he was enjoying himself.

Why Henry?

The question is not what it seems. He is not enquiring why Margot wishes to marry Henry of all people – he banished Margot the moment she began that tedious repetition of her news. He is asking why he himself settled on Henry of all people to be his mental crony. He does not formulate an answer, for it is beyond him to produce a rational explanation for what lies well outside the realms of rationality, but he musters enough mute, instinctive awareness of Henry's role in his mind's life for you to be able to make your own assessment. He needs a Henry as he needs a Yellowley: Yellowley to draw off his natural fermentation of sycophancy, the undistributed accumulation of which might otherwise cause him in mental terms the discomfort of an unmilked cow; and Henry to soothe him with platitudes, to bring a little soporific calm to a mind that in all other respects is about as sedentary as grand opera. There must have been many candidates for the position. He will have favoured Henry because of his slight (as he believed) connection with Margot as an old office colleague. Henry can – could – be trusted, the only one of her male colleagues of whom that may (by Bapty) be said.

And now Bapty does get round to asking the question you originally surmised him to have asked. Since Henry is on the premises of his mind, it might as well be asked now as later, and he does need an answer. For having done some subconscious brooding since Margot dropped her bombshell, he is finding it more difficult to draw comfort out of her preference for a man five years his senior in that it has now dawned on him that the preference excludes not only others but himself. Was Bapty – *is* Bapty – in her eyes so humdrum, so over the hill, so much of a washout, that he is to be regarded as the conjugal inferior of that clapped-out, addle-pated, snot-sniffling, incontinent, half ga-ga old— *Why Henry?*

– Oh, simple, old boy. Father figure.

The staggering, breathtaking impudence of Henry's appearance at the bar of the Broadcasters Club, clutching his tankard and puffing sanguinely away at his pipe as if nothing had happened, so stupefies Bapty that his jaw physically and literally, as well as mentally and metaphorically, drops, to the consternation of the barman who must think him on the verge of an epileptic fit.

Bapty puts down his glass and stretches out his neck, tortoise fashion, to bring his own mottled face to within an inch or two of Henry's mottled face.

– *Piss – off!*

He packs so much venom into the words that not only do his lips move convulsively but spittle dribbles down his chin. The knot of members at the bar, as well as the barman, are now surreptitiously studying him. He will be asked to leave if he carries on like this.

As if aware of the small stir he is creating – though he is not aware – he calls back his unsatisfactorily furious reaction and does it again, a retake, this time with a languid calm fringing on suavity.

– Just piss off, Henry, would you? And stay pissed off?

There was no need to repeat the injunction. Henry is already evaporating like a snowman. He will never be seen again as Bapty's saloon bar pal. His blurred face fades, his check suit crumples inwards and then is gone. Only his beloved tankard remains. Bapty, taking a leaf out of an old Battle of Britain film he has seen, has it put high on a shelf of the traditional village pub in which he has opted to stage this dramatic leavetaking, there to gather dust. And a great melancholy overwhelms him.

He has lost a friend, perhaps his best friend – perhaps his only friend. For who are Bapty's other friends? Yellowley, his self-serving insurance broker? Young Oliver Pease, nearly thirty years his junior? The elusive Ruth, then?

No real friend of Bapty's, the kind of friend every man needs, has entered his mind this whole day long. Perhaps, that, after all, was Henry's main function. How sad.

Bapty finishes his beer. It is fortunate he does not have time for another, for it is unlikely that he would be served it. Remembering the pee he needs, he trudges to the lavatory, feeling sorry for himself.

Wait for Bapty by the door. Let him have this one minute alone with his thoughts.

He re-emerges, perked up a little now, and far from friend-less after all as in his head he calls his good-byes to several fellow-members by name. *Take care, Edgar*, he makes the radio celebrity respond as you follow him down the narrow stairs.

It is just on 4.28. Descending to the Soho street, Bapty tosses away his half-smoked panatella and fiddles with the knot of his tie as he sets about his journey, walking quickly and pur-posefully. Better not let him out of sight.

His thinking is what you might term low-key: all that engages his conscious mind is the task of counting his own footsteps. At 4.29 and a few seconds, on the count of eighty-seven, he turns into Wardour Street. At 4.29 and a half he wheels right into a broad alley. At 4.30 precisely, the time of his appointment, and after walking one hundred and seventy-one steps – an improvement of two on his last performance, he tells himself – he arrives at a door between a theatrical costumier's and a sex cinema, which you may perceive is studded with bell-pushes connecting with the warren of rooms above. Bapty selects the one marked RUTH, MODEL and presses it.

16

This will not do. You should not have come up here with him. The injunction not to let him out of your sight was not meant to be taken so literally. Besides, you know full well that that is not your real anxiety – you could just as well have waited for him outside, there being no other way out of the building. Your anxiety is to have sight of Ruth.

Fortunately the maid speaks no English, so there will be no conversation with her to intrude upon. She has brought Bapty up to a comfortably enough furnished room which with its settee and easy chairs and television set would pass for an ordinary living room but for the absence of knick-knacks and pictures. This is, as it were, Ruth's ante-room. She must be beyond that door there – the only other door leads into a little kitchenette where the maid is pottering.

Let this be clear. Should you follow him when the moment comes for his admittance into Ruth's bedroom, you may consider the novel Edgar Samuel Bapty is living in his head to have come to its final page so far as you are concerned. You would do better to leave now and wait downstairs. When the maid announces him, you are likely to catch only a glimpse of Ruth at best – there will be far more to see in Bapty's mind, afterwards.

There is a soft-porn video tape showing on the TV, its sound turned down. A blonde nymphette reclines in a bizarrely-tilted dentist's chair, her skirt hitched provocatively around her hips while a boy got up as a dentist explores her Venus flytrap mouth with a phallic-looking instrument. It does nothing for Bapty, save reminding him in passing of his own fictitious dental appointment and by association his botched MetCable interview. He does not think of sex; surprisingly, he does not even think of Ruth. He is as detached as if he were in Dr Windows' waiting room, which is, as a matter of fact, where the gaseous after-effects of a pint of draught lager on top of what he has already had have just directed him.

– A much, much better reading I'm happy to say, Mr Bapty. One fifty over a hundred is near enough normal for a man of your age. I'm very pleased with you. Keep it up.

Reassured, he does now turn his attention to Ruth, and aided and abetted by the blonde nymphette, whose writhings still fail to excite him but do suggest anatomical possibilities previously unthought of, tries to imagine her in a variety of erotic positions on a black draped bed. He fails utterly, his mind as unable to focus as when he attempts to shape an epigram or recall the details of an important conversation. He abandons the quest and fills in time contributing to his own obituary, with a passage probably inspired by the surly de-meanour of Ruth's dumpy Spanish maid when admitting him, the irritation caused by which has yet to be erased from his rolling inventory of grudges:

– Before leaving Glassborough Bapty created a local sensa-tion by having a young check-out girl, a school leaver, dismis-sed from the Niceprice supermarket for her failure to smile at him when dispensing change. The Niceprice manager, to whom Bapty had written enquiring asking wishing to know why, given ample choice between pleasant and unpleasant job applicants, he could not give precedence to the former group, was at first reluctant to fire dismiss take the required discipli-nary action. Bapty, however, quoted was able to quote a little-known local by-law by which planning permission for trade premises could be withdrawn where there was evidence of public dissatisfaction with the service provided. Since Niceprice had sought permission to build a car park extend their premises erect a pram shelter—

There are murmurs from the other side of the wall: a feminine laugh, the sound of the landing door opening, muffled good-byes, the door closing again. Bapty pictures an archetypal haunter of canal banks in pebble glasses and soiled raincoat slinking down the stairs. He licks his lips and drums his knees, looking somewhat of the same ilk himself.

The maid should announce him now. But, busy at her sink, she does not. Instead, the bedroom door swings silently open. *Ruth*.

She is all that he has had you imagine – the young, oval face framed by long chestnut hair, the wistful brown eyes, the celebrated sad smile – that elusive yearning quality marred, on this occasion, only by the unlit cigarette in her mouth. She wears an ankle-length wrap-around robe of green cotton which, beyond emphasising her boyish figure, does not set out to add cheap enhancement to her sensuality. It does not need to, for – you cannot but notice – this is a quality she exudes like a scent, as promised by Bapty. Her stockingless feet are sheathed in high-heeled black patent leather shoes – the only overtly erotic touch. She is carrying, somewhat incongruously in the circumstances, a gramophone record.

You must go now.

'Hello, stranger.'

Her voice, which you should not have heard, is pleasant, soft, educated, with nothing of the expected hussiness of her calling.

'Hello, my darling.' Bapty's voice, already naturally high, is unnaturally higher – by far the wrong pitch for heavy gallantry. Standing, he lights her cigarette, his hand trembling a little.

You must go at once.

'What brings you up today, then?'

'Oh, this and that, most of it boring.'

'I wish you'd let me know when you're coming to London, Eddie. I could arrange to make some time and we could perhaps go out for a little drink or a meal.'

'I'd have liked nothing better, my dear, but you see I didn't know how I was going to be placed. I'll give you stacks of notice next time, firm promise.'

'See that you do.'

If you will not go, it is to be hoped that their exchanges are brief and remain on this superficial level. Mercifully, Bapty does not yet seem to have sensed that there is anything amiss. That is thanks not to you but to Ruth, who demonstrably has the gift or power of speedily relaxing him. Tensed up, he would be more on his guard.

So where he is Sam to Margot, Eggo to the shade of Alan Twentyman and the nose-picking petitioners of Glassborough, and Edgar to real and imagined colleagues, acquaintances and fancied acquaintances, he is Eddie to Ruth. Then he does have a friend after all, for their relationship has clearly grown into something more than a mere consultant-client arrangement.

Ruth's affection for Bapty is more difficult to explain than his for her. You are privileged to notice (where you should not be) that as distinct from his mental manner towards her which is unabashedly romantic, his material manner is faintly avuncular. Perhaps, as Henry claimed to be for Margot, he is by way of being a father-figure (though something of an incestuous one in view of the purpose of his visit). At all events, her interest in Bapty is not entirely professional – unless she is a superb professional. And even if that should be the case, he would have been better advised today to have taken Ruth out for that meal and little drink she spoke of instead of wasting his time with MetCable and Margot.

Bapty follows her into the bedroom. You must not go with them. You must leave.

The door remains open. There is a record player on a chest of drawers by the near wall. She places the record she is holding on the turntable as Bapty takes off his jacket and hangs it behind the door.

'Do you fancy a little background music? It'll help you relax.'

'What – music to get laid by? I don't mind.' Bapty, a chortle in his light voice, essays one of the slightly coarse jokes to which he seems partial. 'What is it – the Post Horn Gallop?'

'No, the Pre-Horn Gallop,' says Ruth naughtily, tugging at the belt of her robe.

He knows you are here.

About to close the door, as Ruth's cotton robe falls open and she slips it off her shoulders to reveal a slim, firm body of such creamy perfection that it is astonishing you should only now be receiving your first glimpse of it in over eight and a half hours in the company of Bapty's mind, he looks towards, and through you, and the laugh at Ruth's witty capping of his joke dies in mid-bray.

Who are you? His conscience?

He is afraid. Does a man tremble at what his conscience might know against him? Bapty does.

Can a man close the door on his conscience? Bapty can. His blood at the temperature of chilled wine, he slowly, with a last fearful gape around him, shuts you out of his mind. You hear the key turn in the lock.

You have done all the damage there is to be done here. There is no point in waiting in this room – he will be going out the other way like Ruth's previous client. Nor should you hang around on the landing, for there is bound to be further talk between them as she sees him out. You have been allowed to satisfy your curiosity by seeing Ruth – a good deal more of her, indeed, than you perhaps thought to see – and now you must go down to the street.

Those are the opening strains of Dvorak's New World Symphony striking up in Ruth's bedroom that accompany you down the dingy stairs.

17

He has had time to listen to all four movements by now. You could have gone off and had a cup of tea and a sandwich instead of standing about on the pavement this long.

It is after five now. A middle-aged, rather shamefaced individual sporting a briefcase, after dawdlingly pretending an interest in the theatrical costumier's window, shuffles up to Ruth's doorstep and rings her bell. Another regular, probably – his usual port of call after a hard day at the office. Another father figure even? Will Ruth be as kind to him as she has been – it's to be presumed is even now being – to Bapty? It does not matter. She has been good for Bapty today, that is all that need concern you. He should not keep you waiting much longer.

Presently Ruth's maid opens the door a crack and peers out suspiciously, as she did at Bapty half an hour ago. Recognising the caller she is about to open the door wider when it is wrenched out of her grasp and thrown violently back against the wall of the hallway as Bapty storms out past her, almost colliding with the newcomer to whom he thinks with a snarl:

– *Get out of the way, Prattface.*

He lumbers along the paved alley in a crazy, zigzagging gait, his hands clenching and unclenching, his shoulders heaving, his mouth working furiously.

– *You cowbag! You poxing stinking cowbag! Shut up, you cowbag!*

Ruth's photo-image remains as tranquil as ever in the face of this infantile abuse, as it has every right to do if she understands Bapty's mind at all well: for while it is directed at her it is not aimed at her. Like a believer blaspheming under torture he is absolving himself as he goes along for what he cannot prevent his mind coming out with. *Sorry sorry sorry sorry sorry.* Angrily he rubs a wrist against his eyes where they prick with tears of mortification.

This is your doing. Whatever has happened in Ruth's room, or to face the likely truth of it, whatever has failed to happen in Ruth's room, is your fault. You cannot deny it. Ruth had him nicely relaxed: that is her art, her role, her function, her domain. Yours seems to be the reverse. You, by your intrusive presence, undid all Ruth's work. If Bapty loses you as he charges through Soho, it will be no more than you deserve.

Reaching Wardour Street he stops as one reaching sanctuary, panting heavily. Deliberately to himself, and in solemn, measured tones, Bapty utters:

– Barble. Fastless margin Borrowdale. Gleeb. Tarzan salamander. Lenken proot.

His mind thereby drained of venom like a lanced boil of pus, he proceeds on his way, still at a speedier rate than can be healthy for a man of his weight and medical history, but in a more orderly fashion. Arms swinging now where before they were all but flailing the air, he chimes up in his head to the tune of 'Nymphs and Shepherds' which he has re-set as a march:

– *Shooly Mulligan tim tom tie,*
Tim tom tie,
Wrackly Cooligan him hom hie
Him pom pom tiddle om pie . . .

It has become not so much a quick march as a double-quick march. Bapty has no inkling of what an exhibition he is making of himself as he lopes along the busy street in this manner, his unconsciously military bearing in contrast to the violent, compulsive waggling of his head to mark the beat. All that concerns him is to get away: to get away from Ruth, to get away from his thoughts of Ruth, to place physical distance between his head and what is in it. He will not succeed. Whither Bapty goes, his albatross goes with him.

– *Scarly patterbake tim tom toe tum*
Rickety minchling ho no no,

No-ho no no John no,
No no no Jonathan no . . .

Before crossing Shaftesbury Avenue, uncomfortably aware of having been on the verge of marking time at the pavement's edge while waiting for the traffic to pass, Bapty again stops, and finding the luggage bath lyrics in his head as much a burden as what they were brought in to displace, he verbally though not vocally directs himself, programming himself like a robot that can be controlled by the human voice, or in his case the human thought:

— Shut up.

The directive has a calming effect – too calm, as it turns out, for wafting like a cool breeze into the still, silent mental glade thereby created, comes the comforting voice of Ruth:

— Hey, hey, hey, take it easy! Don't get yourself so screwed up, honey!

Bapty hears himself making a weak, self-denigrating pun turning on *screwed*. He obliterates it with the observation:

— Miffling partisan.

— Don't *worry* about it, Eddie – it happens to the best of us.

— Ample thoroughfare.

— And the more you worry, the more tied up in knots you're liable to get.

— Polldale foalbite.

There is more, which he wants to hear even less. He is powerless to prevent it. He has so cleared his mind that he is out on an open plain with nowhere to run for cover.

— Eddie, love, you know I don't want to turn you out but I'm afraid you're going to have to leave soon . . .

— Coalblock.

— Don't look so woebegone . . .

— Richpeel. *Few business worries that's all.* Tea pork chop.

— Look – really. Next time you come give me a day's notice and let's go out for a nice relaxing meal, then if you want to come back here that's fine, or if you don't feel up to it then no-one's pressurising you, all right?

And all – subtracting only his own shamed responses which he has exterminated with the ruthlessness of a punitive expedition – nicely parcelled up and stored away for him, something to take out and mull over again – and again and again – on a rainy day.

By an unhappy coincidence, it is a rainy day now. Or if it is not, then the snow is melting on this fine September evening, for water is dripping from a crack in the ceiling of the little semi in Glassborough. Bapty, swinging down Charing Cross Road towards Trafalgar Square, marks the drops as they land in a red plastic washing-up bowl. *Parp. Parp. Parp. Parp.* If he hopes this ploy will keep the ensuing scene out of his head, he is mistaken. His *parp parps* serve only like the ringing tone of a telephone to connect him with his sulky-faced second wife Juney. They are in bed, she in a tamely-provocative black see-through nightie, he in striped pyjamas. Both are pretending to read. There is a long silence – twentieths of a second tick by. Now resigned to playing out what in his drained state he is powerless to prevent being played out, and wishing to get it over with, Bapty in London at last prods Bapty in Glassborough into saying:

– All right, then tell me this. If I've got problems in that direction as you're suggesting, how is it I never have any trouble managing it with Ruth?

– Who's Ruth when she's at home?

– Never mind who Ruth is for the present. Just take my word that keeping it up is the least of my worries.

– Don't be cruder than you can help, Edgar.

You realise, do you, that this discussion cannot have taken place? Study Juney's face, it being clearer in Bapty's mind's eye than is his own. She is of an age more or less with him, but here she is presented in her early thirties, as he must be too. That would make Ruth about fourteen years old.

He may be talking to Juney but in the reality of his head he is talking to himself, to persuade himself that the recent fiasco with Ruth, as it must have been, was a one-off, an isolated failure – though *If you don't feel up to it then no-one's*

153

pressurising you did rather carry the hint of this probably not being the first time on record. But whether it was or no, he wishes to believe it was: and so why should he be so anxious not to hear what he has just said?

The scene is not over, that's why. Let Juney continue – unless Bapty can muster the resources to prevent her doing so:

– And I never said anything about you having problems in that direction as you so delicately put it. We already know what your problem is, Edgar – you just don't want a family, do you?

He has fallen into a trap – allowing Juney to use his own much-needed reassurances to himself as bait. *National pomegranate, luggage bath, croolferble spherical objects*, retorts Bapty. But Juney is not so easily deflected.

– Oh, I see! The great Edgar declares the subject is closed, so the subject is closed! Not for me it isn't, Edgar. If you didn't want children you should have come out and said so before ever we got married.

– Arkansas barrow-tuft.

– Never mind not wanting them yet, you don't want them ever. I know, you, Edgar. And it's because of that you've put yourself off making love.

– Moccasins.

– Yes it is. You can say you haven't but you have.

– Cardboard box.

– Because you quite rightly associate making love with making babies, and you shrink from that in every sense of the word, don't you? You don't want anything to do with responsibilities, do you? No – you think you're the big I Am but I'm sorry to say you're very immature, really.

– Quite the little home psychologist, aren't we?

– And I'll tell you something else while we're on the subject, Edgar. You were just the same with Pam, weren't you?

Was he? All the rest rings true but would Juney really have dragged his first wife into it like that? Or is he just permitting her to do so, encouraging her to even, to evade having to go through the same tiresome business again with Pam?

154

Bad luck, Bapty – here comes Pam now, in her ridiculous outfit of swimsuit, Miss Glassborough sash and beauty queen crown. Archly simpering, she is showing off her wedding photographs, though to what audience is not spelled out. *And this is one of Edgar picking his nose . . .*

Feeling distinctly martyred – such bizarrely damaging cameos, Bapty feels strongly, should be the stuff of dreams, not waking reveries – he crosses Trafalgar Square, heading for The Mall. He must be bent on walking to Victoria, though no such decision has been monitored. The exercise would do him good if only he were not pursued by demons – he is like a man with a wasps' nest about his head. Why are Bapty's womenfolk persecuting him so? At least Margot is leaving him well alone for the present. Or perhaps he is leaving her well alone, and these others are taking the opportunity of occupying, like squatters, the vacuum created by her enforced absence.

To his relief, as he reaches the Park, several aspects of the environment demand his attention. Shoving a panatella into his ruminating mouth he fires off a broadside to *The Times* on the case for putting park benches on the same hourly hire basis as deckchairs, to discourage a yobbish public from stretching out on them full length like so many down-and-outs. He breaks off from time to time to remind any bearded passers-by he chances upon of the regulation requiring all those enjoying the Park's amenities to be clean-shaven.

– Oh, but you're quite right – somebody's got to have the courage to stand up to them. I only wish you'd come round and have a word with my postman. I've often wanted been on the verge of telling him to take my letters away again and come back when he's smartened himself up a bit . . .

It sounds like Henry but it can't be. Henry's barred for life. Bapty's companion in the Victoria Station bar is his brother Donald, whom he doesn't even like. Is dreary Donald the best substitute he can field? He's tired, that's what it is.

Still, it all gets him along his way without further recourse to more damaging, wounding personal material, though the end of his panatella is in rags from the intensity of his cogitations.

He flings it into the gutter as he steps off the kerb in the course of describing an elaborate arc around a pavement newspaper stand, the better to avoid the reproachful eye of the one-legged paper seller from whom he has occasionally bought a *Standard*, and who might therefore be chagrined at his neglecting to buy one now. Cursing the fellow for imposing on him so, Bapty heads for the Victoria Station bar, where his brother by now having finished his pint and gone, he commences to knock back brandies by himself.

It wants twenty minutes to the next Portsea train. Bapty's exertions have left him with a stitch in his side, for which he blames the human race. Taking his theme from a wall poster advertising special trains to a jazz festival, he composes not so much a hymn of hate against jazz, folk singers, buskers, beards, students, student grants, teachers, and an ever-widening periphery of ancillary subjects, as a magnificent Hallelujah chorus of sustained and bellowing rage.

Bapty is fairly drunk as he meanders along to platform nineteen where his train is now waiting. Come with him if you will – his day is not over yet, his novel still unfinished. The state his mind is already in, it is affected little by his excesses; its owner, though, is by now a little more likely to say what he thinks as well as think what he would like to say. In the crowded commuter carriage where he has found a seat, such a prospect could be alarming, were he not so physically tired. Having halfheartedly picked a quarrel with a swining pig-faced snot-gozzling ticket inspector who is probably not even on the train, Bapty yawns and closes his eyes.

His last waking thought is how fervently now he wishes he had let the one-legged newspaper vendor sell him a *Standard*, so that when the mean bastard reading his own copy opposite should ask if he might please have a glance at his paper, Bapty could remark – as indeed he does anyway:

– Oh, I'm sorry – if I'd had I known you wanted to read the paper I'd have bought stopped off at W. H. Smith's and bought an extra copy. Unfortunately however just so happens bramble perkin don't just happen to be a pigging free travelling public library soap nails garble buy your own pigging luggage bath . . .

Bapty's head jerks like that of a man hanged. His mouth lolls open. He snores. Let him sleep now. Bapty's dreams are out of bounds.

18

He's surely not proposing to drive in his condition, is he?

Yes, he is, but only in his head, fortunately. Swathing ticket collectors, porters and railway clerks before him, Bapty stomps out of the station, bobbed on a tide of commuters, his teeming head but one of a sea of teeming heads, his storm-tossed mind only one among many, his seething thoughts but droplets in a Severn Bore of thinking that comes roaring out into Station Approach, across the Harbour Mall shopping precinct and down along all the winding streets of Portsea with each hourly train.

The swining bloody-minded pig-faced snot-gobbling car park attendant who refused to give Bapty change for the pay-and-display meter this morning is no longer on duty. As Bapty locates his Ford Capri and checks the door-locks, the long-term parking permit in his windscreen establishes to your satisfaction that he did not need change in the first place. He probably never asked for any. There is no evidence, even, that the disobliging attendant even exists. That does not save him from a further tongue-lashing before Bapty drives off – though not in his own car. He prefers a broken-down old Cortina a few spaces away, the attraction being that it is hemmed in by a badly-parked station wagon. In a sequence of spectacular reverse and first gear manoeuvres, Bapty uses the Cortina as a battering ram to slew the station wagon out of his path. He tucks a rude note under the offending vechicle's windscreen wipers and drives off at speed.

Refreshed after his nap, invigorated by his car park adventure, Bapty strides briskly along the empty brick mall of the shopping precinct where everything is closed at this hour except an incandescent Wimpy Bar, and down open concrete steps into the High Street, livelier with its pubs, amusement arcades and fish and chip cafés. Bapty fumes at the lights for unduly favouring the cross traffic, though anyone actually driving would regard them as being at green, then puts down his foot and makes for South Portsea at a steady forty. His brother Donald, straitjacketing himself into his safety belt, puts forward the view that forty being a sensible, realistic speed for town centres, it is time it was made law. Bapty feels a pang of regret at no longer being able to offer a lift to old Henry.

As the manager of the local radio station, it's only to be expected that Bapty should be quite a well-known figure in Portsea. He likes that: after a day in London, as he reminds Donald – or is reminded by Donald, it's not clear which – it is a relief to get back to one's own little cabbage patch where everybody knows everybody. It pleases him to be greeted or smiled at by his small-town acquaintances every fifty yards or so. Some he runs over, others he pauses to have a word with. *If you don't like the programmes why do you listen to them all day long, you stupid mare?* Some of the arcades and cafés he closes down, others he burns down. It is good to be home.

Passing the *Chronicle* offices at the bottom of the High Street, he actually does stop and speak to someone, a plain, plump woman in her forties, searingly identified by Bapty as the paper's radio and TV writer. A detrimental article on Portsea Sound's output flashes up on his mind's microfilm viewer as he shakes hands. They exchange a few pleasantries, the offending columnist never suspecting that in the minute and a half before the station manager of Portsea Sound moves on with a cheery wave, she has invited this valuable contact to dinner, he has accepted, arrived at her home with a bouquet of flowers and bottle of wine and consumed a three course meal, and now over the coffee and mints is affably informing her:

– Ah, well, since you ask, Lucy, no, as a matter of fact I didn't enjoy it one little bit. In fact I'd go so far as to say it was just about the worst pigging dinner I've ever encountered. Would you believe I give my dog better meals, out of a tin, than that boeuf Stroganoff roast rack of lamb chicken casserole I'm still trying to keep down . . .

It is evident that his dinners with the *Portsea Chronicle*'s critic are among the social highlights of Bapty's year. It really is heart-warming to see him so cheered up after such a day. He is back where he belongs now, with all these fresh Portsea thoughts to think, so very many of them clamouring for attention before the night's sleep claims him, that the ones that have been troubling and tormenting him all day recede and vanish. It is as if Ruth, Margot, Juney, Pam, Jepcott, Dr Windows, have all been put away like toys.

Turning out of the High Street into Fishgate, where the shops gradually give way to offices and commercial buildings, the sight of a Kentucky Fried Chicken house reminds Bapty that notwithstanding the unspeakable dinner he has just had (it was quite palatable if the truth be known), not to mention his two lunches in London, he has yet to decide on this evening's eating arrangements. Driving still at a steady forty ahead of his own pedestrian progress, and now divested of his brother's company, Bapty sees himself dowsing the lights of his car where he has parked it on the cracked concrete drive of his little bungalow and slipping his Yale key into the lock of the wired-glass front door with fingers made greasy by the parcel of Chinese food he is carrying.

It is the first time you have seen inside Bapty's bungalow. It is a cheerless sight. Doubtlessly it is to enlist his own sympathy towards himself that he exaggerates the squalidness angle so – the unmade double bed with its one grubby pillow, the cups and plates stacked in the sink, last night's drained wine bottle and sticky glass still on the coffee table, the brimming ashtrays etcetera: surely he has a cleaning woman to deal with all that? But it is the clock-ticking, clammy silence that is so depressing. No wonder Bapty's spirits slump. Feeling queasily ill, he advises himself firmly, *Bite over at Winnie's.*

Getting out of the car just now – he gets out of it again, to remind himself what all this is about – he has covertly noticed the woman next door, she of the dog turd incident, squinting disapprovingly through her net curtains at his arrival home with the brassy, barmaidly-looking woman he is now with, doubtless picked up later tonight in Winnie's Bar. To cheer himself up he sends his prying neighbour a poison pen letter. He does not actually compose it – it may be one he has composed already – but has her tearing open the envelope with trembling hands and reading it where she has picked it up off the doormat in her bare little hallway. It is something about her being known to consort with tramps and meths drinkers under the pier, the smellier the better. *Wellwisher*, as he signs himself, is his new chirpy self again by the time he reaches the one lit building among the tall empty warehouses and abandoned canning plants down at this end of Fishgate.

In fact the white fluorescent lights account for only the first two floors of only about a third of a building, Portsea Sound being a much more modest establishment than Bapty – possibly influenced by the spaciousness of MetCable's premises upon his arrival there this morning – gave it credit for when considering the conversion prospects of this old fish warehouse with his managing director Lance Barrington. You will have to tread carefully here, not knowing the lie of the land. If Bapty is dropping in to see how the day has gone and what problems may have cropped up in his absence, there could be members of his staff, Oliver Pease and others, buttonholing him on every corner as he does his rounds of the studios. You do not want to put him off his stroke by butting into any of these confabulations when he may have to make snap decisions – this is Bapty's livelihood, don't forget. You have seen for yourself today how unlikely he is to find another place.

The corner door of plain glass beneath the Portsea Sound blue neon logo is locked. As when he reached his bungalow a few moments ago, Bapty lets himself in with his own Yale key, and climbs the two or three steps past a commissionaire's cubby hole, which is unattended. Surprisingly, he has nothing to say to its absent occupant – perhaps he is saving his energies for bigger fry.

Indeed he is, and as he moves across the tiny lobby and swaggers through double swing doors into a sizeable open-plan office area with smaller offices leading off it, he is already in full spate:

– Jesus Christ Almighty, can I not turn my back for one single swining day? Look at that pigging clock, Oliver. What does it say? It does not say two minutes past eight, it does not say eight on the dot, it says two minutes to eight precisely. At two minutes to, Oliver, we do not have the Rolling pigging Stones, we have the two-minute pigging local news round-up. Now find that piss-gargling Lionel Valentine and fetch him to me . . .

The office area, though brightly lit, is empty of life, as are all the smaller offices, their doors wedged open by wastepaper bins against the advent of the cleaners. Typewriters are covered, coat pegs bare. The place seems as forlorn, with only Bapty in it, as did the empty bungalow to which he must return tonight. It has that kind of night emptiness where the fluorescent lights could be heard buzzing, were it not for the telex machine chattering to itself in fits and starts beneath the staff notice board by the far doors, and the loudspeaker outlets in the walls vibrating with the sound of the Rolling Stones. It is, as Bapty has pointed out, not eight o'clock and not two minutes past, but it is not two minutes to eight either. It is six minutes to. As the record is faded out, a pleasantly slangy voice, typical of commercial radio, recognisably sober and presumably that of Lionel Valentine, announces that that was 'I Can't Get No Satisfaction' and that his next choice will bring it up to time for the local news and weather. Bapty meanders across to the telex machine, frowning conscientiously as he scans its billowing printout but registering only the words *Vatican spokesman* and *premium bond winners*, perhaps for his luggage bath collection. Glancing just as unproductively at the busy notice board, he passes through the nearby swing doors into a corridor. His manner is aimless: it is plain that he need not have come back here tonight. No wonder he doesn't feel stretched, as he may or may not have told Ralph Jepcott.

Stop. There is something he has not seen here. It is a folded sheet of memo paper with his name scrawled on it, pinned to the board. Can it be important?

Reading Bapty's mail would count as intrusion under the rules but reading his messages is probably in order. It gives a London number, and the message, *Mr Bapty – pse ring before 8*, followed by the scrawled initials of the person who took it down. The call is not identified by name – it's to be assumed that none was volunteered – and the number would mean nothing to the Portsea Sound staff. It will, however, mean a great deal to Bapty, should he get to see it, as it does to you. It is Margot's private line number, which he got from her operator this morning.

What can she want? Only Bapty can find out. How can he be told? He cannot – not by you. Pin the message back on the board and hope that he sees it. *Ring before 8* – the time she will be leaving the newspaper office, you may suppose: they keep late hours. It is now just over five minutes to.

Pushing through the swing doors, you are just in time to see Bapty turning down a flight of steps at the end of the short corridor. Keep him in sight – this is a ramshackle sort of building full of unexpected doorways and turnings where you could lose him like a rabbit down a hole.

A red ON AIR light winks on and off above the door at the bottom of the steps. Peering through its thick porthole window into the small studio, you can see Bapty talking to a shirt-sleeved young man wearing headphones whom you must surely recognise, having seen him naked in bed with Margot as well as, almost as memorably, lurching drunk over in Winnie's Bar. Bapty, affability itself, appears to bear him no grudge. He moves through into the producer's control box, leaving Valentine sitting at his microphone shuffling his notes with one eye on the clock. You may go in now.

The studio clock's red second hand is sweeping round towards four minutes to eight. Bapty, observed through the picture window that takes up one wall of the studio, chats to the bearded man at the recording and sound control consoles –

another familiar face: you have seen him often in Winnie's Bar – while signing a sheaf of dockets or whatever they may be – an administrative chore that should it occupy him for the next two minutes, will leave him trapped in the control box until Lionel Valentine has read the news. It will then be after eight, too late to ring Margot even if he should see the message.

Perhaps it is not important. There is nothing to be gained from worrying about it, since there is nothing you can do. Instead, take the opportunity to contemplate Edgar Samuel Bapty behind his glass wall as you might a zoo octopus in its tank.

Studying him with the sound off, so to speak, you see just a thick-set, middle-aged, nondescript man in an absurdly tight suit of creased blue velvet, dishevelled, gritty-eyed, a little the worse for drink, stifling a yawn and mechanically signing dockets. Cut off from his thoughts, there is nothing about this man to give you pause. You may retort that there has been precious little to give you pause even after eleven hours' continual and total access to his thoughts – yet pause you did, and pause you do. True, you would perhaps have had a more fruitful, profitable day of it inside the mind of a scholar, a scientist or a poet. Bapty's mind, by contrast even with the lowliest schoolteacher, laboratory assistant or hack, has squandered and frittered this day away. No, he has not written *Paradise Lost*. He has not split the atom. Yet he has been on such journeys and seen such things today in his head that a man would wish to tell his grandchildren about – if only he could remember a tenth of them. Blessed forgetfulness is already descending like a fog on his day's memories, swirling all but the sharpest and cruellest into the mists of time.

Bapty the man has achieved nothing today, and Bapty the mind learned nothing – except raw information on which to feed and fester. Little that could be classed as constructive or useful has been engineered in that head of his – no good or pious thoughts, few insights, no regrets. Of his rages and fearsome revengeful tableaux, the best that may be said is that they are at least exuberant. He has added not a jot to the sum of human happiness – neither his own nor, as far as can be seen, anyone else's. Yet, discounting only himself as being as much the victim of his own lack of any sense of proportion as the dodo of its lack of ability to fly (but what would Bapty do with a sense of proportion?), he has harmed no-one either – except vicariously. Living, or rather thinking, vicariously, is perhaps after all Bapty's one abiding weakness. It is a trait which he who lives a novel shares with those who read it.

He has finished his business here now and after a pleasantry or two waddles out of the control box and across the studio just as the producer raises a finger to cue Lionel Valentine into his news round-up. The ON AIR light glows steadily red as you follow Bapty out of the studio. It is two minutes to eight precisely, as he claimed it to be four minutes ago. Retracing his steps along the corridor, back towards the office area where he must pass the notice board again, he may yet see Margot's message in time.

He does not get that far. He reaches a solid-looking door half way along the corridor, knocks, and opens it. You have seen him pass through this door before. Its legend in gold letters reads L. M. BARRINGTON, MANAGING DIRECTOR. Like all the other offices at this time in the evening, Barrington's is empty. But not to Bapty.

– That seems clear enough, Lance. Thank you for spelling it out. My resignation will be on your desk first thing tomorrow morning . . .

Oh, come along, Bapty! The notice board, man! He has one and a half minutes.

– No, I'm sorry, Lance, allow me to correct you. It's not a question of principle, it's a question of policy. Is the station manager in charge of deemed to be in charge of the day-to-day running of the station this station Portsea Sound or is he at the beck and call mercy every time you crook your little finger because I'm sorry to say this, Lance—

See that other office door across the corridor, propped open like all the others, save the managing director's, with its occupant's wastepaper bin. See the name of the occupant in gold letters: E. S. BAPTY, STATION MANAGER. See the small heap of letters on his desk. He is bound, when he has done fulminating on the threshold opposite, to wander into his own office and at least leaf through them.

Has Bapty, if he has done nothing else, amused you at all today? Then you do have a chance to be of service to him after all. There is a minute and a few seconds yet in hand. Go to the notice board, take down Margot's message, and place it on top of his pile of letters. Hurry. Then cross your fingers.

19

It cannot be very far away. It is the local pub for Portsea Sound and you know that it is either on the sea or very close to the sea. Fishgate runs down to the harbour. It must be around here somewhere.

There it is – the low tumbledown structure of hanging tiles and weathered boards on the corner, its inn sign creaking in the evening sea breeze. The Taps. This side entrance, with CIGAR DIVAN engraved on its ornately bevelled window, and PRIVATE BAR on the old splintered door, must be Winnie's Bar, where the Portsea Sound people congregate. That is where he will be found when he has finished at the studios. Or you must hope he will: it was certainly his promise to himself earlier. There seems no reason why his phone call to Margot should deflect him from coming to the pub – the reverse, if anything. That's if he's managed to get her. You were wise to leave when you did. His heart was thumping so as he picked up the telephone that sensing your presence might have had serious consequences.

Go round to the harbour entrance. You will recall that the front bar overlooks the back one across the bottle-cluttered central bar counter. Near enough to hear Bapty's thoughts, when he arrives, but too far away to hear what he is saying, especially through this convivial hubbub.

It is like a tapestry come to life. All the familiar faces are here. There, a bit more mature in appearance than Bapty portrays him, is young Oliver Pease, talking to a very attractive secretarial type who when last seen was stumbling out of his bathroom during that Christmas party, having monopolised it for so long that Bapty was reduced to peeing in a vase. Lionel

Valentine is on duty of course, but there are the two colleagues who were with him the night he was so drunk that Bapty had to read the news himself, thereafter coming down into Winnie's Bar where having accepted Valentine's congratulatory scotch he then fired him. All the rest you have seen at various functions, Bapty's leaving parties and other jollifications. The distinguished-looking man in the camelhair overcoat, standing rather apart from the throng in earnest conversation with someone who looks like his accountant, is of course Portsea Sound's managing director, Lance Barrington, to whom Bapty has just been tendering his resignation. And the man he is talking to, you probably now recall, is one of his co-directors who was present at the board meeting when Bapty recommended Oliver as his successor.

Here on your side of the bar, briefcase at his feet, large scotch at his elbow, the sharply-dressed, sharp-featured Yellowley, chin every bit as blue as Bapty painted it, gazes across at this gregarious little gathering with the undisguised covetousness of a small boy peering into a sweetshop window. It is apparent that to everyone except Bapty – or even more exclusively, Bapty's mind – he is as much an outsider here as his patron was in the Broadcasters Club. Can it be that in plying him with cigars and standing him slap-up meals at the Captain's Table, Bapty's mind is revealing that its owner feels sorry for him? But before the notion that the abrasive interior of Edgar Samuel Bapty may conceal a heart of gold runs away with you, look now upon The Taps' beefy landlord as he emerges from his cellar, wiping his powerful hands on a glass-towel. Where have you seen him before? Yes: he is the chief torturer and leading assassin of the League of Justice.

There is a slight stir among the Portsea Sound crowd as the plush curtain masking the street door billows. Imperceptibly, they make a path for Bapty as he enters, rubbing his hands against the evening chill, puffing furiously at a glowing panatella, and inwardly smirking. Oliver Pease comes forward with an interrogative tippling gesture, inviting him to have a drink. Someone else signals the substantial lady who must be

the eponymous Winnie, but it is the League of Justice execu-
tioner in person who comes forward to serve Bapty. He must
be gratified by all these intimations of respect.

That must remain an assumption, however, for it would be
difficult at present to isolate any one thought or impression
from the dozens coursing through his head. His mind is going
like a dynamo. It is exactly as it was when he emerged from
Jepcott's office having arranged to superimpose one lunch
appointment upon another – the same kind of jumble of
attempted mental shorthand deteriorated into scribble.
*Scratchback following shingle hark-plate steam-point
elephant Cartwright mangle* ... But no, not quite exactly.
Bapty was not smirking, then.

His first articulate thought since entering the pub, as he
sights Lance Barrington and the other director, now expresses
itself over these elated burblings:

– *Shit.*

The exclamation, or rather its cause, has the effect of partly
disciplining and organising his mind to the extent that it now
compartmentalises itself into three. It cannot entirely turn off
the tap of Bapty's exhilaration – perhaps it would be dangerous to try – and so the smaller of the three segments is allowed
to go on prattling to itself – *nutmeg person fillblow wallowing*
– like a child left in a crèche, while the other two apply
themselves seriously to the tasks in hand. One, reluctantly
acknowledging the necessity of social intercourse with the
Portsea Sound managing director, is hastily drawing up a
schedule of likely observations, interjections and asides
tailored to put their presenter in the best possible light, while
the other – and again this is strongly reminiscent of those
confused moments after Bapty came out of Jepcott's office – is
over-excitedly trying to get an itinerary of some sort together:

– Eight twenty just make it nine twenty-five cab meet no said
not half nine Majestic get there what nine forty champagne
Mrs Jepcott meal in suite maybe ring first check could be nine
twenty miss eight twenty hour to wait bugger it change
mind ...

Mrs Jepcott, was that? It will untangle itself soon enough. For the present, though, threading his way across to his masters, Bapty is obliged to interrupt himself there and give priority to the range of professional smalltalk he has got lined up, commencing with:

– Oh not bad, had lunch with Margot for old time's sake she's getting married again did I tell you dropped in the Broadcasters few old faces no I don't think you'd know him rather a rich gentleman by all accounts who can blame her what kind of a day has it been here. . . ?

While not saying any of this he has taken possession of the glass of white wine proffered by Oliver Pease, who now tactfully retires from this august senior company. Civilly raising his glass in a sweeping gesture to his staff in general, and accepting their congratulations on his honourable resignation, Bapty catches the eye of, or has his eye caught by, Yellowley here in the front bar, who is raising his own glass in just the same manner as Bapty when trying to ingratiate himself with that famous radio personality at the Broadcasters Club. With a nod and a fuzzy smile, Bapty perhaps restores any faith you may have lost in his irascibility by thinking at Yellowley:

– Piss off.

He pays proper attention to what his managing director is saying to him, selecting his responses from the over-profusion ticker-taping out of his mind: *Yes. Yes. Yes. Yes. I could have told* you *that, my friend. Did he? Was he? Has he? Then he's a pratt of the first order first-rate pratt. Yes. Yes. Yes. Bollocks. Spherical objects of the most rotund variety.* The other director now joining in, and the conversational load being spread somewhat, it becomes safe enough for Bapty cautiously to re-open the other section of his mind containing that bewildering itinerary. This time he takes it more slowly:

– All right say she makes the eight twenty gets in nine twenty-five otherwise nine twenty gets in ten twenty-five says sod it Mrs Jepcott check with desk . . .

Mrs Jepcott again. But it begins to make sense now – except that it makes little sense. To summarise: Margot might just manage the 8.20 train, failing which it will have to be the 9.20, unless the prospect of cooling her heels at Victoria for close on an hour puts her off the whole idea. She doesn't wish him to meet her at Portsea station and so he will have to check her arrival with the Majestic Hotel reception desk. A suite has been booked under the name of Mrs Jepcott (is all this a joke, Bapty's mind taking itself off on some mad, elaborate prank?) and champagne already been ordered. Ten minutes or so after 'Mrs Jepcott's' arrival, he will join her in her suite, where they will discuss supper . . .

Has Bapty departed from his senses? Can he be serious? Certainly he sounds so: there is no hint of idle wishful thinking here, no pipedreams – on the contrary, all these arrangements are very hard work indeed for Bapty's mind. He is not doing this for fun.

Then it follows that the crudely-expressed invitation to Margot which he tried to expunge after that shared cab-ride to Cambridge Circus truly was issued – though more elegantly put, it's to be hoped – and however she may have snubbed him then, as he thought, she has had a change of heart since. Hence the phone message to which you so cleverly drew his attention. Had you not done that, then who knows but that—

Listen. She is speaking to him.

– Didn't know quite how seriously take you lunchtime . . . all we put away quadruple Armagnacs God's sake . . . if *did* mean it, Sam . . . Auld Lang Syne and all that . . . does so happen I've remembered some unfinished business down in Portsea . . .

He is replaying only the highlights, of course. You may depend upon it that a faithful, notarised transcript of the entire telephone conversation is safely lodged in Bapty's mental archives waiting upon detailed analysis at his mind's leisure – say the moment Barrington clears off. Meanwhile, for Bapty, *Does so happen I've remembered some unfinished business down in Portsea* has already taken on the imperishable familiarity of the prayers and multiplication tables he learned by rote at school in Bradthorpe. What a pleasant change for Bapty to have something agreeable embossed upon his brain for once.

He skims over the Majestic Hotel arrangements again, directing himself as executive to employee *Not look watch* in case of the important consequence that Barrington might think him tired of his company. Upon the next service message, however, *Buy bugger drink*, Barrington looks at his own watch and to Bapty's relief drinks up and leaves, taking his fellow director with him. It is just coming up to 8.20. Margot, if she has made it to Victoria on time, should be sitting on the train by now. Bapty, turning to join the now-thinning Portsea Sound contingent, has her running for it.

Signalling to himself *Better get round in*, he relays the same signal to his League Of Justice confederate with a circular motion of the finger. Yellowley is not included. Perhaps Bapty will buy him a large drink some other time – in his head.

Having to respond now only to the chitter-chatter and gossip of his youthful staff, Bapty's mind for a spell has so easy a time of it that it begins to indulge itself, permitting not only the opening shots, as it were, of the forthcoming Majestic Hotel episode where he and Margot are easing themselves into the desired mood with a glass of champagne (though she does cause him a twinge of anxiety by appearing in Ruth's green cotton wrap-around robe), but also a fanciful account of his adventures in London:

– I'll tell you who I had quite a chat with today – in fact had lunch with him had a drink with him bumped into him at the Broadcasters Club: Ralph Jepcott, the top man at Metropolitan Cable. You know how they used to talk about steam radio, the system we have now will be known as steam TV when that lot get in their stride, I know one thing, young Oliver, if I were your age . . .

Another twinge of anxiety: this time at the mental mention of Jepcott. Bapty's mind conducts a lightning court of inquiry into the cause of it. Its findings are that it is centred on the Majestic Hotel booking, which for reasons yet to surface is in the name of Mrs Jepcott.

Maybe Bapty fluffed his lines when ringing Reception and they suspect that all is not above board? If he did, he can soon put that right. He rings Reception again:

– Majestic oh yes Portsea Sound here Edgar Bapty my name would you have one of your seafront suites available yes it's for one night Mrs Jepcott J – E – P—

No, all that seems to have gone smoothly enough. His mind double-checks and reaches a more circuitous conclusion. It is the mechanics of getting up to 'Mrs Jepcott's' suite unnoticed that is causing Bapty the trouble.

Although he has claimed to Margot – or claims to have claimed to Margot – that the Majestic is under new management, that may not be true; and even if it is true, it is no guarantee that he will not be recognised. He is well-known in the town. Sweat beads Bapty's forehead for the nth time this day as the hotel's revolving doors pitch him into the seething melee that is the Portsea Conservative Association's annual dinner dance. At every step, under-managers, reception clerks, barmen, waiters, porters, lift attendants, bellboys greet him by name. Mrs Bapty, he is informed leeringly, has just gone up . . .

A tic of spite twists Bapty's face as he pays for his round of drinks. *No skin off my nose*, he tells himself with unconvincing piousness. *That cowbag's lookout, not mine.* He at once dismisses the thought, if not as unworthy then as inappropriate to the occasion, and coaxes the Margot of *Does so happen I've remembered some unfinished business* back to her suite, this time minus Ruth's wrap-around robe.

– So how's it all gone today, any snags, hiccups or cock-ups. . . ?

– So how's it all gone today, anything I should know about, Oliver, don't tell me if there is. . . ?

– So how's it all gone today. . . ?

He is feeling queasy again. It must be the excitement, or the anxiety, or a mixture of both. The white wine can't be helping, either. That is his third glass.

This is not very nice: Bapty is objectively considering the case for vomiting. He pictures himself doing so, in what looks like an exceptionally seedy outside lavatory situated in a small cobbled yard. You do not have to look: starting, or if you will finishing, with those pre-lunch sherries, which he seems to wish to take most of the blame, there is a good deal to come up.

He continues to size up the pros and cons. It would take the dead weight off his stomach and tone up his system ready for a light tête-à-tête supper with Margot, but what about the aftertaste? *Mints*, thinks Bapty, and glances towards the display card of little packets he has half-noticed by the cash register. They are raisins.

He cancels the urge to be sick but continues to brood on the state of his mouth. Perhaps he should go home and clean his teeth, and shave, take a bath and change while he is about it.

It would be a good idea, Bapty. A better idea than the one he now puts into practice on the basis that his nausea is caused by hunger: namely, to order two cold sausages and accept a further glass of wine.

– So how's it all gone today, the usual crackpots ringing in, I suppose. . . ?

By way of a diversion, Bapty takes over the afternoon phone-in programme and deals with one or two of the offending crackpots himself, so peremptorily and brutally that his lips jerk as he ostensibly listens to the bar chatter. Realising for once that he is doing it, he makes an elaborate performance of working his jaw about, to suggest that he is suffering from whatever mild complaint may be surmised from these manoeuvres.

Time passes. Practically the whole Winnie's Bar scenario so far, minus the initial luggage bath ravings, is now repeated and re-repeated in Bapty's mind, much of it embellished, some of it curtailed. The drinking school slowly breaks up until only young Oliver Pease – perhaps out of duty – remains to talk to him, then he too is gone. It does not matter one way or the other to Bapty. He continues:

– Reception oh yes this is Portsea Sound here my name's Bapty that's right I wonder if you could find a suite for tonight for one of our guests yes Mrs Jepcott's the name J – E – P—

Yellowley has long ago departed, his exit unheeded. He looked a little hurt, perhaps not appreciating how royally he has been entertained today, before being put away in his box.

Bapty has several times consulted his watch, on each occasion subtracting the current time from Margot's projected checking-in time. The hour, after too many glasses of white wine and panatellas, is here at last. The blazing bungalow in his mind signifies that he is about to use the payphone out in the tiny passage. He pushes his half-full glass towards the beer-pumps, an indication that he does not propose to return.

It is quite chilly now, with a stiffish breeze coming up from the harbour. Shivering on the corner, uncertain whether the passage leads out to the front or side entrance, you are alerted in due course by intermittent through prolonged retching noises from behind the high flint wall of the yard and outhouses adjacent to the pub, into which is let a door labelled GENTLEMEN in gothic letters. There must be another entrance to the yard from the passage where Bapty has been telephoning. Presently he ventures groggily into the street, dabbing his mouth with a handkerchief and looking quite pale and ill under the sodium lamplight. Dr Windows issues a curt warning which is even more curtly repudiated.

Has Margot arrived? Yes. He has a kind of newsreel of her doing so, getting out of her cab with her overnight bag and handing it to the hall porter. Irrelevances such as how much she is giving the driver and whether, if she is wearing gloves, she removes one or both before signing the registration form, crowd his mind. They continue to occupy him as he sets off around the harbour to the fairy-lit promenade, his shoulders hunched against the wind. Such is the wealth of minutiae issuing from Bapty's tingling brain – it must be a device to keep him calm – that by the time he himself has arrived at the hotel, some ten minutes' walk away, he has got her only as far as the lift.

The familiar revolving doors deposit Bapty in the familiar lobby, now looking quite bare without its usual brigade of dinner-jacketed and ballgowned Portsea Conservatives, and the staff on duty markedly reduced to a receptionist and a porter reading a newspaper. No-one recognises Bapty as he walks across to a house phone and speaks into it briefly.

Running his tongue across his teeth, and issuing an urgent instruction to raid Margot's toothpaste while in her bathroom, he now approaches the lift by which she has ten minutes ago or ten seconds ago, depending on which account you go by, ascended. Bapty thinks, as he steps into it and presses the button for the fourth floor:

— Welcome to Portsea. Well, I think champagne is called for, don't you?

The lift gates close and Bapty whistles through his teeth and rocks gently on his heels as the indicator lights jump from one to two to three to four . . .

Where do you think you are going?

20

You may believe you have some right to be here, having been in your small way instrumental in bringing these two together. You have no such claim.

Besides, you are wasting your time. Bapty is not going to say anything to Margot that he has not thought already. If anything – and if he is wise – he will say a good deal less.

As to their purpose in being here, you have already been told all that you need to know. There is a point at which curiosity becomes mere voyeurism, and you reach that point as you cross this threshold. Go away. Edgar Samuel Bapty may be living a novel but he is not living a pornographic novel. If you want to see that sort of thing there are cinemas that cater for such tastes.

It is not very interesting, you know. Hear what he thinks as she admits him into the sitting room:

– *Striped wallpaper.*

And as he notes that she is still wearing the black suit she had on at lunchtime – her professional uniform, it must be, although she has changed her white high-necked jumper for a crisp white shirt:

– *Always togged up like a pigging widow.*

If he has not thought this gallantry already today, you know well enough by now that it is the kind of thing Bapty's mind comes out with. There will be no surprises here. You may as well occupy yourself elsewhere. Go home and read a book.

Bapty thinks:

– *So . . .*

– *Here we are again, then . . .*

– Welcome to Portsea . . .
– Luggage bath. Hello then . . .
Bapty speaks:
'Hello then. Welcome to Portsea.'
'It doesn't change, does it?' says Margot. She sounds a little breathless.

You have been in their company seven seconds now. It is enough. You do not want to listen to this smalltalk. Please feel free to leave.

Bapty thinks:
– Champagne.
Bapty says:
'Ah, the champagne *has* arrived. Good.'
'Yes. It was already here. Nice and chilled.'

Very well. You are here, you will not leave, and you cannot be made to leave . . . except by Bapty, if he finds you here. You know the rules. If you choose to disregard them, that is your affair. He does not yet know you are here but if he should get to know – should you infiltrate yourself into his consciousness, as you know you must not – then you are on your own. Who knows what Bapty might not do, should he stumble on you here?

Sit quietly, then. Do not breathe.

It is a big, high room with tall windows, all warmly curtained. Wallpaper in pale Regency stripes, as Bapty has noted: gilt-framed mirrors, prints of old Portsea. Two matching chaise longues with a big square coffee table between them. Easy chairs, a desk, a TV set. A side table with glasses and champagne in an ice bucket. Bapty takes all this in and fixes on the bedroom door, which is ajar. He thinks *Bathroom.*

The bathroom will be beyond the bedroom. Not that it is any concern of yours. The other side of that door is forbidden territory to you.

Margot sits on one of the chaise longues, creating for Bapty the immediate three-prong dilemma of whether he should sit next to her, opposite her, or in one of the chairs by way of a compromise. His mind struggles with the problem while he

178

takes the champagne out of the bucket and struggles with its foil. *Once broke nail like this*, a memory cell pipes up helpfully as he completes the operation.

'So we eat up here?' says Margot.

Bapty's response is automatic, after his recent internal upheaval: *Feel sick*. Carefully, he rehearses his reply:

– *Yes, I thought we would. I thought we would, yes. I thought we would, why not?*

He says:

'Yes, I thought we would, why not?' – during which he has been thinking:

– *Nowhere else to eat round here after all too late.*

He adds:

'There's nowhere else to eat—'

Let's face it, his mind has prompted him. '—let's face it,' he concludes.

Margot picks up the big padded menu from the coffee table and scans it idly. *Pigging cork*, thinks Bapty.

'Can you manage that?' Margot asks as he puffs and blows with the bottle between his knees. His mind drafts a brief acknowledgment which his vocal chords deliver, while Bapty in a deeper seam of thinking, thinks:

– *Not feeling too clever tell the truth.*

That is another speech draft, just a rough working text to have by him in case he is obliged to leave his meal or can't finish his wine. Bapty is indeed distinctly under the weather, not surprisingly after all he has put his system through today. According to the readings you are getting he is feeling nauseated again, though not as much as when he was in Winnie's Bar: his scalp, armpits and crotch feel as if they have come out in a rash, he still has a heavy sensation in his stomach, and the exertion of opening the champagne bottle is darting his chest with twinges.

Dr Windows pays a house call.

– *More than a question of diet, Mr Bapty . . . Whole lifestyle . . .*

Although he cannot help thinking, out of habit, *Spherical*

objects, Bapty for once keeps the observation to himself. To Dr Windows he acknowledges:

— *Yes, have been overdoing it a bit.*

The admission makes him feel better. A resolution: tomorrow he will start looking after himself. He feels better still. Bapty, but for his aches and pains, is on top of the world again.

'Now we both had steak for lunch . . .' muses Margot, browsing through the menu.

He promptly feels sick again. He says: 'Yes, something light, I reckon.' Too quick for his mind, apparently: trailing behind him it lamely reports what he has said:

— *Yes, something light, I reckon.*

He eases the cork into a napkin with a plop, and champagne fizzes over his hand. 'There we go,' says Bapty. *There we go*, records his mind, taking it all down. He feels terrible. He thinks:

— *Don't drink top up glass all bubbles pour in bucket bathroom throw up oh Jesus God sweat green bile might hear shut bedroom door toothpaste clean teeth finger deodorant spray armpits try have quick crap . . .*

If it was a seduction scene you were hoping for, you must be sadly disappointed.

He carries the two glasses of champagne across, Margot's brim full, his own, as directed, being two-thirds froth. He urges himself to sit next to her but ignores the advice and takes the armchair at right angles to her chaise longue.

About to raise his glass, Bapty thinks:

— *Here's to our project.*

Raising his glass, Bapty says:

'Here's to our project.'

'I shouldn't be here,' says Margot. She is not the only one.

About a minute has gone by since you barged your way in here on Bapty's heels. Another five seconds are now occupied by Bapty smiling at what Margot has said, pretending to sip his champagne but shrewdly not doing so, and thinking what to say next.

'Well, then,' says Bapty at length, having received his instructions.

'So what's this Mrs Jepcott lark in aid of? And who is Mrs Jepcott?' asks Margot.

'First name that came into my head,' says Bapty, repeating what he has been told to say.

'Well, it makes a change from Smith, I suppose. But I meant why all the elaborate precautions – aren't we getting a bit long in the tooth for that kind of thing?'

Bapty thinks:

– *One of us might be, but I'm quite sure the other one's still got a fair way a good way a long way to go, you stinking cowbag. Depends what kind just what kind of thing you're talking about have in mind, my love.*

Bapty says, with something like coyness in his light voice:

'Ah, now that depends what kind of thing you have in mind, my love.'

'I didn't mean *that*, you fool,' blushes Margot, coquettishly coy herself. To which, in a complete change of tone and with a complete change of approach, she then adds with a direct simplicity which carries overtones just as erotic: 'I meant why do we have to make a game of it? I was once fond enough of you to want to marry you – I'm still fond enough of you to want to sleep with you. You invited me, so I'm here.'

Bapty thinks:

– *Yes, I see you are, you poxing cowbag. That's all it pigging needs with you, isn't it – one pigging invitation. I bet if the Yorkshire stinking Ripper had got you on the phone and said how about it darling you'd have been on the first pigging train to Leeds wouldn't you you stinking cowbag. Thank you.*

Bapty says, with quiet dignity:

'Thank you.'

He makes a decision, which he follows up, to bring the champagne bucket over and place it on the table, telling himself, or trying to persuade himself, that it will be easy to tip his wine into the bucket whenever Margot is not looking. Poor

Bapty: he looks at the end of his tether. It is a wonder that Margot does not remark on it.

Money, he has thought, together with some attendant administrative details, while crossing the room. Now, topping up her glass, he says, a touch awkwardly:

'Oh, by the way – money.'

'What – to tuck in my stocking top?' says Margot archly.

Bapty entertains a saucy image of her doing so as he says: 'Rail fares etcetera. Expenses. Though it'll have to be a cheque, I'm afraid, if that's all right by you.'

'What – don't I have to put in a claim form?' teases Margot. 'I wish you were my features editor.'

Bapty says and thinks, simultaneously – in respectively wry and bitter tones:

'But not your books editor.'

– *But not your pigging books editor.*

'Yes, well *he* doesn't pay my expenses and I don't expect you to,' Margot says lightly, not rising to the bait.

Bapty toys with the wounding notion of visualising Margot on a dirty weekend in Brighton with Henry, but he too decides not to rise to the bait . . . just yet. Meanwhile he has commenced to think what he now commences to say:

'At least let me take care of the room. Just sign the bill and I'll grab it when it comes through to Portsea Sound. That's one reason for the Mrs Jepcott stunt, by the way.'

'You mean someone might have thought 'Ello 'ello 'ello, he's had his ex down for a bit of slap and tickle?'

Bapty sketchs a pleasurable account of them doing just that in Winnie's Bar, and puts it aside for further development.

'You know what they're like, that lot.'

'Would you have minded? Or might it have queered your pitch with whichever mysterious lady friend you're not telling me about?'

– *Mind your own business, you cowbag. I'd like to queer your pigging pitch, by Christ I would. It'd be funny if Prattface found out, wouldn't it?*

'I was more concerned with not queering *your* pitch, actually. I mean if it should reach certain ears.'

'It won't,' says Margot succinctly.

– No, I bet it pigging won't.

She adds, toying with her champagne and carefully not looking at him: 'By the way, it's understood this is a one-night stand, to use a revolting expression. It's not going to be a habit.'

'It was at one time.'

– Why not? It always pigging used to be.

Margot, little realising that the observation was meant to be almost as spiteful as the thought that fathered it, misunderstands. 'With us? Not as much a habit as it should have been, I'm afraid. But we won't talk about that.'

Bapty doesn't want to think about it, let alone talk about it. 'Where does old Henry think you are?'

– Luggage bath.

'Does it matter?' shrugs Margot.

'Not really. Just anxious on your behalf, that's all.'

– If it doesn't, why are you marrying the poor sod?

'You needn't be.'

'No, I'm sure.'

– No, I'm pigging sure I needn't be. You've had enough practice after all, haven't you? You bloody two-timing cowbag.

Margot, with a little reprimanding sigh, says: 'Now what's *that* supposed to mean, Sam?'

'Well, you've had enough practice after all, haven't you?'

Ruefully, swirling her champagne around the glass, Margot says: 'I suppose I asked for that.'

They are getting into deep waters here, and you with them. You should not be listening to any of this. If Bapty even suspects—

He does. It is as if his brain has missed a beat. Astonishment, it looks like, lights his face. He claws at his throat.

'Are you all right, Sam?'

'All right – champagne down wrong way.'

That's not what Bapty's mind says. Bapty's mind says that he is feeling decidedly odd. But at least, and it is not after all because of you. It is physical – a sensation of *wooziness*, he informs Dr Windows, replenishing his own champagne glass as well as Margot's. Bapty must expect sensations of wooziness, the way he maltreats himself.

He repeats the question he mentally put to her over lunch at Mrs Grundy's:

– *You tosspotting bloody cowbag – come on, then, how many have there been?*

But in modified form:

'You know, I still don't know to this day how many there were, Margot.'

Put like that, it doesn't seem to offend her. In amused tones: 'Not as many as you like to think. Where *do* you suppose I found the energy?'

With simulated bitterness towards himself Bapty says: 'Not from the same source I got mine, such as it was, that's for sure.' You know it is simulated, for having instructed him what to say and how to say it, his mind is now hissing venomously, *Tell the cowbag you understand . . .*

'Look, it's all water under the bridge now, love, but I do understand. I mean, I know I gave you a hell of a hard time.'

Margot gives a little shrug of her mouth, and tilts her champagne this way and that. 'As you say, water under the bridge . . .' She drains her glass. 'I wish we could have talked like this when we were married, though. Well – not necessarily like this – just *talked*.'

'That was my fault.'

– *We'd nothing to pigging say, had we?*

'And mine.' This time Margot pours the champagne.

– *And look where it got us when we did talk.*

'The only time we did talk properly it resulted in my dragging you down here. Biggest mistake I ever made.' *Total twat of myself*, he continues, unknown to Margot.

'Oh, you don't know, Sam . . . Let's say it needn't have been.

Now that *was* your fault, pissed out of your skull every night.'

Bapty throws back his champagne in one. It sears his throat like molten glass. There is no uplift: exhaustion is soaking into his bones. He feels as wretchedly tired as if he had been up all night. *Bed*, he thinks – and as if magically granting him the first of three wishes, his mind at once deposits him in bed with his first wife Pam. It must be the first time you have seen her not wearing her Miss Glassborough sash – certainly the first time you have seen her not wearing anything at all. She has an enquiry.

– Can you answer me one question, Edgar? Why ever did you bother pulling me when all you're good for is pulling your plonker?

– *Silly bitch. By-flung. Rockwall. Carryplane. Day-drop.*

'You know,' says Bapty, having been surreptitiously fed his own next enquiry during this interlude. 'I never did find out who it was down here.'

'Who says there was anybody?'

'There was though, wasn't there?'

– *Don't give me that, you lying bitch, or I'll knock your pigging eyes out.*

'For a while, when I was deeply unhappy.'

'Who?'

– *Oliver Pease, Lionel Valentine, Lance Barrington – all right, who else?*

'Does it matter, Sam?'

'I'm curious. Was it anyone on my staff?'

'No, of course it wasn't. What do you take me for?'

– *A cowbag.*

Bapty himself doesn't reply.

'It wasn't who you're thinking,' says Margot, believing erroneously, it would appear, that she can read his mind (she would have a shock if she could). 'It was someone at the Sailing Club, if you must know.'

A miniature portrait gallery, like a mounted collection of cigarette cards – Margot's Lovers, A Series Of 50, perhaps – fills Bapty's mind as he asks: 'Who at the Sailing Club?'

Margot has had enough of all this. You cannot blame her – this is not why she came down to Portsea.

'Oh, really, Sam! Look – are we going to order that meal or not?'

'*You cowbag!*'

He has said it. He has spoken it, blurted it out. It was bound to happen – while you should not have heard any of this, you are not to blame. It is as if Bapty's mind and Bapty's voice have been playing one of those parlour games where certain words must not be spoken, and Bapty's voice has been caught out. As it had to be, of course – it is a game that Bapty's mind could not lose.

It has little impact on you, for you have been hearing it all day, but see the impact on Margot. She looks as if she has been slapped across the face.

'*What* did you just call me?'

Alarm swells through him – quite literally swells, it feels like: a sensation of balloons being pumped up inside his body. He gasps, exhaling painfully as if he could expel his panic like gases.

He knows you are here.

'*You pigging, poxing cowbag.*'

He intones it absently, calmly, routinely, dispassionately – he does not mean to say it, he has no wish to say it, he does not know he is saying it. He has simply, in his terrified preoccupation as he stares at the space you occupy, left the gate open and let his mind out to wander where it will.

'You're pissed, Sam.'

How much have you heard? How much do you know? Who, what, are you?

Margot is on her feet. 'Sam, I came here tonight because I thought after seeing you in the jittery state I found you in at lunch that you needed a little help from a friend. I'm afraid I was optimistic. You need a lot of help and I can't give it.'

He stares and stares, not hearing Margot and not hearing what his mind replies aloud to her:

'*You've destroyed me, Margot, do you know that?*'

186

'You've destroyed yourself, Sam, if anyone has. I'm going to pack.'

He sees you. As Margot stalks into the bedroom, and the two of you are alone together, you materialise yourself to him. He sees you – perhaps as a ghost, perhaps in the solid flesh, you are not to know, but he sees you. He points.

– *Who are you?*

He wants to speak to you but his roaming mind fails to act on the request. He clutches his shirtfront as pain like a steam-iron singes his chest. He is trying to pull the pain away like a hot poultice. His brain becomes a pin-table of lights and jangles. He cries out. Margot is at the bedroom door, alarmed.

'What's wrong?'

She hurries over to him, yanks his tie loose, absurdly pulls his shoes off, feels his brow, his pulse, his heart. This disorganised concern will not make him better.

'Shall I get a doctor?'

The pain is so intense now that it transmits itself raw, untreated, to Bapty's brain. He knows now that he is having a heart attack for his head is having a heart attack too.

He cannot speak – but his mind can. Aloud.

'That'd just suit you, Margot, wouldn't it? Whisk him into the pigging hospital, then no-one's the wiser. Sorry, my love, not this time. I'm going to die and you're going to be found here with me, caught with your knickers down for once. And try keeping that *from Prattface.'*

'Don't be silly and don't talk. Do you have a doctor in Portsea yet?'

Bapty does not answer. He has some thinking to do. The pain, miraculously, is lifting, as a cloud lifts. It is there still, it has not gone, it will not go, but it is as if it is suspended in air, like one of his thoughts. He feels it yet he does not feel it. A peculiar sensation: but it allows him to think. Perhaps that is the idea.

He is no longer afraid of you. It is clear that he still does not know who you are but he does not care who you are. He has become as incurious about you, even less curious about you, as about his fellow-patients in Dr Windows' waiting room.

Dr Windows is not in attendance now. Too late for that.

Bapty is thinking, in a mellow sort of way, about his impending death. Calmly, unhurriedly, he ponders whether he ought to commend his soul to God. He concludes that he could not in all conscience bring himself to do so, for it would make his last act on earth a self-seeking and thus spurious one – it would be like trying to sell himself an insurance policy, like that little pratt Yellowley.

You would never have accused old Bapty of honesty, would you?

That matter settled, he reviews his life as far back as this morning – a fair sampling, you may be sure, of the whole. He has no regrets that he can think of save one – he should not have sent that poor little girl to Borstal for dropping her chocolate wrapper. Even though he quashed the sentence later he does regret that, bitterly.

'Tell her I'm sorry,' mumbles Bapty.

All this has been in the time it has taken Margot to cross to the desk and pick up the telephone.

'What, Sam?' Then at the phone: 'Come on, come on, come on . . .'

Bapty chuckles in his mind, and out loud his mind says: 'Too late, my little fruity one, you've had it!'

The cloud of pain is more distant now, and another cloud is here to carry Bapty away with it. But not yet. With all the strength left in him, using it up as a thrifty person will use up the last scrap of soap, he raises himself from his chair and points at you. He roars, though it comes out only as a croak:

'And you're a bloody witness!'

Contented now, he lies back and murmurs, in his head, an absolution. *Publico status quo cumulus inglorius quantum theory magnificat luggage bath* . . .

Edgar Samuel Bapty dies, a reasonably happy man.